WANTED WED OR ALIVE

THYME'S WEDDING

MELISSA F. MILLER

BROWN STREET BOOKS

Published by Brown Street Books.

Brown Street Books ISBN: 978-1-940759-51-7

CHAPTER 1

White Sands National Monument,
outside Alamogordo, New Mexico
Thyme

I'm standing, barefoot, in cool, white gypsum sand, holding a waxed plastic saucer sled. The afternoon desert sun beats down on my shoulders, but, somehow, the sand beneath my feet doesn't absorb the heat.

Victor pushes his sunglasses up to the crown of his head and squints at me, grinning. "You ready to lose?"

"Not a chance, Callais."

I situate my sled on the peak of snowy sand and sit

in the plastic circle. I arrange my legs lotus-style and lean forward over the front edge of the sled. Beside me, Victor lowers himself into his saucer and scrunches his legs up in front of him, knees to chest.

Amateur.

His weight is distributed all wrong. But that's not my problem.

"Ready?"

"I'm ready." I flash him an intense look.

"On the count of three. One, two, three!"

We push off and careen down the dune. Well, *I* careen down the dune. When I reach the bottom and tumble, breathless and laughing, out of the bright orange sled, I look around for Victor. He's stuck a third of the way down the hill, beached in the sand.

I double over with laughter while he scoots himself toward the bottom, pushing with both hands.

"You're not exactly aerodynamic," I tell him once I've caught my breath.

"You cheated." He stands up and wipes the sand from his palms.

"I did *not*!"

I swat at him with my free hand, and he catches it, pulling me close to his chest. I nestle in, trash-talk forgotten, and tilt my chin up so I can meet his eyes.

"Wanna kiss a winner?" I offer.

A slow smile spreads over his lips, then he takes me up on my invitation.

As he covers my mouth with his, I think—for at least the hundredth time—what a great idea this road trip was.

I'll be honest, I wasn't sure what to expect when he asked me to join him on a cross-country trip. He was assigned a series of articles on the economic situation in towns throughout the South and Southwest and thought it would be fun to drive across the country as he reported on the issue. He invited me along.

Summer in New York City is steamy, stinky, and stale. You can quote me on that. Because I'd already decided not to take summer classes, I didn't have school to worry about. My biggest client—media mogul Cate Whittier-Clay—shares my opinion of summer in the city, so she, her husband, her daughter, and their nanny (Victor's sister Helena) fled Manhattan for the French countryside until the beginning of October. She set up an online video classroom environment so she and I could continue her personal training sessions remotely, and she encouraged me to make it available to my other clients, too.

So, there was quite literally nothing keeping me in the city. And my boyfriend was offering me a once-in-a-lifetime vacation. Even though I didn't know what I was getting myself into, I packed my bags in record time.

And now, here I was, digging my toes into the world's largest known deposit of gypsum sand thanks to Alamogordo's desert climate, which prevents the salt from evaporating. I mean, we're sledding. In the desert. In September.

I giggle at the absurdity, and Victor pulls his head back to search my eyes.

"You're having a good time."

"I am. And not just because I kicked your sorry butt," I tell him.

"I'm glad." He releases my hand and digs into the pocket of his khaki shorts.

"Me, too. This is … perfect. You, me, and the endless New Mexico sky."

His grin turns serious. "I like the sound of that. You. Me. Endless."

A weird, tight note creeps into his voice. I furrow my brow. What's he up to?

He fumbles in his pocket for a moment, and then a small, velvet box appears in his palm. He pops it open and I glance down at it. The sun glints off the ring inside the box, and I have to look away.

"Thyme, will you—"

No. No, no, no. Please don't.

I don't say the words, but I'm thinking them as hard as I can. Surely the message will get through by telepathy or osmosis or … magic? He can't ask me to marry him. He *can't.*

"—marry me?"

My brain goes on the fritz. I stare at him, feeling fuzzy and numb and abjectly miserable, for the longest minute of my life.

I study his face. His warm brown eyes. The scar near the corner of his full lips. The curl of hair that insists on trailing over his forehead no matter how much hair pomade he uses.

His eyes are locked on mine. Waiting.

I love him. I love him more than I imagined it was possible to love another person. Every day is better because he's in it. He's smart, sarcastic, kind, funny, generous, and gorgeous. He'll make a great, thoughtful partner and, someday, an involved and loving father.

And I've known for a while, or at least suspected, that this day was coming. He's dropped plenty of hints over the past year, and his interest in matrimony really ramped up after the second of my two sisters was married last fall.

Finally, I find my voice. "I'm really sorry. But … my answer's no. I can't. I can't marry you, Victor."

His expression shutters, and he snaps the ring box closed.

Suddenly the heat feels oppressive, smothering.

He drops his gaze from mine. After a moment, he clears his throat. "Let's return these sleds to the ranger station and go get some lunch. How's that Mexican place in town sound—the one the guard at the missile testing ground told us about?"

His voice is level and impersonal. That fact, more than anything, is my undoing. My eyes fill with hot, fat tears and I stare down at the orange saucer sled by my feet, watching it blur and undulate as I try not to cry.

When I have a handle on my emotions, I raise my head. But he's already trudging across the sand, headed back to the rental jeep without waiting for my response. I swallow hard around the lump in my throat and set off behind him. My heart's hammering wildly.

I can almost hear my sisters. *Thyme, what have you done?*

WE RETURN THE SLEDS TO THE RANGER STATION IN silence, brush the gypsum sand off our feet in silence, and drive to the adobe restaurant in silence.

After the waitress seats us and brings us each a glass of water and a laminated menu, I crack.

"So, what? You're not going to speak to me for the rest of the trip? Maybe I should get a flight back home."

Victor looks up in surprise from his phone, which he's been fumbling with under the table ever since we were seated.

"What? No, I …." He trails off and places his phone facedown on the table. "Sorry, I was texting your sisters."

I goggle at him. "You're *kidding*. Right?"

If anyone is going to seek sympathy from my sisters, it's going to be me. Although, truth be told, I'm not so sure either of them will understand.

He gives me a sad smile. "I had to tell them the surprise party's off."

I'm still reeling from the engagement ambush, now he's talking about a surprise party.

"What?"

"I stupidly assumed you'd say yes. So, Sage and Roman and Rosemary and Dave were planning to meet us in Vegas the day after tomorrow to celebrate."

Ooof. My stomach seizes like he's delivered a gut punch.

"Victor—"

Just then, the waitress reappears with a basket of hot, greasy tortilla chips that are obviously housemade and an array of salsas.

"Gracias," Victor says in a solemn tone that manages to be totally polite while at the same time conveying 'we're in the middle of something here.'

She nods and glides away, quickly and quietly.

I toy with a chip, breaking it into pieces.

"You were saying?"

"I want to explain—"

"You don't owe me an explanation, Thyme."

The pain in his voice drags my eyes away from the chip crumbs falling onto my plate and up to his face.

"Yes. I do. I love you."

He narrows his eyes. "But you're not *in love* with me?"

"No!"

The only other couple in the restaurant both turn to look at us.

I lower my voice several notches. "That's not it. I *am* in love with you. I want to spend the rest of my life with you."

"Then I don't understand."

I reach across the table and cover his hand with mine, holding my breath and hoping that he won't yank his hand away. He doesn't.

I exhale. "I don't think we should get married."

"Yet, you mean?"

"No, ever."

"You don't want to be married?" He tilts his head and studies me.

"No. Well, that's not true. I *do* want to be married. To you. I just don't want to *get* married."

He shakes his head, a blank, confused look in his eyes. "I don't follow."

"What happened at Rosemary's wedding?"

He purses his lips and thinks. "Your sister and Dave were married. You and I danced until dawn. Sage and Roman got engaged. I met your parents."

"Before all that."

"I don't know, Thyme. A lot happened."

"Yes, you do know. Rosemary was *abducted* by a loan shark and held captive in a storage container. My parents were *arrested.*"

He frowns.

"Mmm-hmm. And what happened at Sage's wedding?"

Understanding lights in his eyes, but he pretends not to know what I'm driving at. "Sage and Roman were married. You and I danced until dawn. Your parents were furloughed from prison so they could be there."

"Did you forget Sage's house was vandalized, her dress was caught up in a bankruptcy, her rings were stolen, she needed stitches, and, oh yeah, she fainted?"

"In fairness, that all happened *weeks* before the wedding."

"Sure, I'll give you that. And, in fairness, none of it would have happened if they hadn't been getting married."

I wait for him to try to argue the point, but he shrugs as if to say I'm right, but so what?

I sip my water and wait for him to catch up. The liquid is cool as it travels down my throat, but the glass is sweating in my hand. Or maybe my hands are sweaty. It's hard to tell.

"Wait—that's why you don't want to get married? Because your sisters' weddings hit a few snags?"

His incredulous expression is something out of a poorly done high-school play: broad and exaggerated. I try to stifle a laugh and fail.

"A few snags? I think you mean a series of catastrophes, disasters, and dramas."

"Thyme, all that matters is they were married at the end of the day. I mean, isn't that the point?"

My laughter dies as tenderness swells in my chest. Yes, that is the point. And, at the end of the day, I do, very much, want to marry Victor. I just don't want to have a wedding.

I catch my lower lip between my teeth, thinking.

"What?"

"What what?"

"I know that look. You're devising something."

"Not devising ... just ... do you really mean that?"

He squeezes my hand. "Of course I do."

I put down the glass and fill my lungs with air, then let out a long, slow breath. "In that case, Victor Callais, will you elope with me?"

His expression stays neutral but he blinks. Once, twice.

"Elope?"

"Yeah," I say, warming to the idea that only crossed my mind for the first time less than thirty seconds ago. "I mean, we are heading to Las Vegas after Arizona. Unless romantic comedies have lied to me, we can get married there, easy peasy."

"That's true."

"And Sage and Rosemary and the guys were already planning to meet us there."

"Also true."

"So, what do you say?" My building excitement screeches to a halt. "Oh, wait. That's not fair. Your family ...."

He flashes me a smile. "My family will understand. Traveling from Brazil to the States for a wedding would be an extraordinary cost. I mean, don't get me wrong, my parents would gladly do it. They adore you. But, my extended family ... it would be a hardship. A lot of them would have to miss it, and they'd be disappointed. But if we elope, then there's no wedding bad luck to worry about, right?"

"That's the idea."

"So we could have a big party in Brazil, after we're married?"

I consider the idea. "I don't see why not. Oh, but what about Helena?"

His sister can't go back to Brazil. It's not safe for her.

He cocks his head. "Surely we can also have a big party here, too, afterward. Invite our friends from the city and your extended family to the Resort by the Sea to celebrate? After your parents are released from prison?"

My enthusiasm bubbles back up to the surface. "That would be perfect."

"So, what do you say ... the day after tomorrow, we find an Elvis impersonator and tie the knot at some all-night chapel before gambling the night away?"

"Um, no. More like find a justice of the peace, have

a quiet garden ceremony, then go someplace fancy for dinner with my sisters and their husbands."

"Details, shmetails."

"Did I just agree to not one, but two, wedding celebrations?"

"Basically. A master negotiator, you're not."

He leans across the table and kisses me, trapping my giddy laughter in my throat. I kiss him back hard.

He's wrong. I've negotiated myself right into the perfect scenario: I get to marry Victor without worrying what tragedy will befall my wedding day. No reception means no chance of bad luck. I'm sure of it.

I'm also wrong. Dead wrong, as it turns out.

CHAPTER 2

Sage

I'm staring down at the text from Victor, frozen with disbelief, when the phone rings in my hand. I pull down the notification bar. It's Rosemary.

Of course it is.

"What's up, Rosie?"

"What's up? What do you think, Sage? I'm calling to see how Chip did in the golf tournament? I'm calling about Thyme!"

I catch Roman's attention and roll my eyes.

"Okay, jeez. You don't have to freak out on me. I'm not the one who just turned down a marriage proposal."

Roman puts down the magazine he's flipping through. He's not a regular reader of *Southern Style,* but this month's issue includes a feature on Chip, Muffy, and their kids. Half-brother Roman rates a mention as Chip's caddy, but the biological relationship was apparently a bridge too far for the magazine. He doesn't seem to care. I'm just glad that I managed to hide the jelly stain on Skylar's dress before the photographer snapped the shot. Nanny win!

My favorite caddy leans across the breakfast bar and plants a kiss by my ear. "And thank goodness you didn't."

A smile plays across my lips. Marrying Roman was the best decision I ever made. My smile fades as I return my attention to Rosemary and our baby sister's boneheaded decision.

"Have you talked to her?" I ask.

She sighs. "No. I … thought she might call you. You're …"

Not so bossy? I think. But what I say is, "Closer in age? Easier to get ahold of?"

"I was going to say 'less bossy,' actually."

"You were?"

"I know who I am, Sage."

"You're bossy in a *good* way."

That characterization earns me a laugh. "Now you sound like Dave. Maybe you should give her a call."

"I guess." But I have to wonder what you say to someone who's just crushed a guy's heart?

"Do you have any idea why she'd tell Victor no?"

"No."

"Neither do I. I don't get it. She's making a mistake."

I tend to agree. But the difference between me and Rosemary is that I would never dream of saying as much to Thyme.

"We don't know, Ro. She's got her reasons, I'm sure. And our job is to support her."

Rosemary grumbles something indistinct. I choose to interpret it as agreement. That's another difference between the two of us. What can I say? Sometimes it's easier to go along to get along.

"Have you cancelled your flight yet?"

She switches gears so abruptly that I feel dizzy. "What? No, Victor only texted us two minutes ago."

"Good. Don't."

"Don't what?"

"Don't cancel your flights. We need to go out there and intervene."

"You want to ambush them in Vegas and try to convince Thyme to marry Victor?"

"Yes."

"No."

She huffs. "Why not?"

"Where to start? It's not our business, for one."

"Of course it's our business. She's our sister, Sage, and she—"

My phone beeps, two quick sounds. *Bip, bip.*

"She's calling me."

"Take it. Call me back."

Rosemary hangs up before I can respond.

As I swipe the screen to pick up the incoming call, I glance at Roman. He shakes his head and pours himself another glass of iced tea. He's mildly to moderately amused by my sisterly drama, as usual, but I know he also feels awful for Victor.

"Hey, Thyme," I answer with as much warmth in my voice as I can. No matter what, she could probably use a friendly ear right about now.

"Hi!" she chirps back, entirely too cheerfully.

Even if she doesn't know that I know, shouldn't she be exhibiting some sadness here? If not sobbing, then at least a mournful tone, something? Unless, of course, she really *doesn't* love Victor …

Not possible. I've seen her with him. I've heard how she talks about him.

"Are you okay?" Maybe she's having a breakdown.

She giggles. "I'm better than okay—I'm getting married!"

I have no idea how to respond. Finally, I manage to squeak out, "Who's the lucky guy?"

The line goes quiet.

"Thyme?"

"It's Victor, you goofball. Who do you think?"

"I don't know. I'm so confused. Not ten minutes ago, he texted me and Rosemary and said that you rejected his proposal."

"I did! But then I proposed to him—well, kinda, sorta. It's a long story. But we're eloping."

"You are?"

"Yes, we're getting married the day after tomorrow."

I struggle to catch up. "In Las Vegas?"

"Yep."

"And you want us to be there, right?"

"Sage! Why would you even ask that? Of course I do."

Roman wrinkles his forehead and shoots me a bewildered look. *Tell me about it.*

"I don't know, Thyme. It's all so confusing. Why did you say no in the first place?"

I hear her big inhalation of breath. Then a whoosh as she lets it out. "It sounds silly, but ever since you and Rosemary had your weddings, I've been dreading a big wedding with a ceremony and a fancy reception. Not that they weren't beautiful—they were. I mean, that beautiful meadow and all the blue glass and yummy food, but—"

"Will you spit it out already?"

"I don't want a big wedding. It's not really feasible for Victor's extended family to travel here; and Mom and Dad, you know ..."

"They could try to get a set of day passes, like they did for my wedding."

"I know. But, I don't want the fuss. I'm afraid something will go wrong."

"Lots of things will go wrong, Thyme. That's life."

"Yeah, I guess. I just don't want the drama."

To each her own. "Okay, so a drama-free elopement it is. All that really matters is you and Victor starting your life together."

"Exactly."

I can hear the relief in her voice. And there *is* something romantic about the idea.

I go on, "I guess as an added bonus, Rosemary and I don't have to throw you a shower and wear matching dresses."

She snorts. "See, everyone wins."

I hesitate. "Well, everyone but Mom and Dad. And Victor's parents. Thyme, are you sure about this?"

She waits a beat before she answers, but when she does, her voice is firm and clear with no trace of doubt. "I'm positive. Like Victor said, we can have two parties later. One in Brazil, probably in the winter, and one here, after Mom and Dad get released."

"Okay, if that's what you want."

"It is. I don't know how to explain it, but I feel like a weight's been lifted off my shoulders. Ever since your wedding, I've been carrying around the grim thought of having a wedding of my own someday."

She's so deeply weird, but she's my sister, so I accept on face value that the prospect of a wedding strikes her as grim. But I need to know *why*.

"Why, though?"

"I can't explain how I know it, but I know if I plan a wedding reception, something terrible will happen. I can *feel* it. It's bad juju."

"Now you sound like Mom," I tell her.

"I don't care, Sage. I'm being serious. It's been a dark, ominous cloud, following me around."

The shudder in her voice is like a glass of cold water. There's nothing funny about this to her.

"I'm sorry you've been feeling that way. Why didn't you say something?"

"Like what? I'm glad you and Rosemary found the men you want to spend the rest of your lives with, but the idea of getting married horrifies me."

Okay, she has a point. That announcement wouldn't have sat well with me, and it would've gotten Rosemary all riled up. I glance over at Roman who appears to be absorbed in some esoteric golf statistics he's pulled up on his laptop.

Still, I pick up my mug of hibiscus tea and slide open the door to my small balcony. After I close the door and settle into one of the bright pink Adirondack chairs, I lower my voice and say, "You're positive that it's the idea of a wedding that horrifies you, right? Not being married to Victor?"

She's been clear about it. But still. This seems like the sort of possibility a person should probe, repeatedly, from all angles, before eloping. I hold my breath and hope she doesn't bristle at the question.

Luckily, Thyme seems to understand my reason for asking. "I'm one hundred percent sure. I know it's the wedding, not the groom. That's why I've been so stressed out. I know I want to be with him, I just didn't see a way to avoid the whole wedding thing. Running off to Vegas to get married is the perfect solution!"

The dread that filled her voice moments ago

vanishes, leaving behind no trace. I have to smile at the sunny way she sings the words.

"Great. I'm so happy for you. Do you need me to bring anything?" Like what, I can't imagine. The idea of getting married on the spur of the moment is antithetical to my love of planning and organizing. I wouldn't be able to do it. Even thinking about it is making my palms sweaty.

"No, thanks. Well, actually, yeah. I got a call from, Mr. Doolittle, the property manager at my building—"

"Doolittle?"

"Yeah. He said I've got so much mail piled up that my mailbox is stuffed and the postal carrier has filled two of those big plastic bins. The building management told him he can't leave it behind the desk anymore, so I asked him to send it to you. He sent me the tracking; it'll get there today. I'm sure it's mostly junk mail, but will you flip through it and bring along anything that looks important?"

"Of course. But you didn't stop your mail?"

"I didn't think I needed to. I do all my banking and stuff online. I don't think I've gotten more than a handful of mail the entire time I've lived in that place. I'm serious."

"That's so weird that you have this avalanche of mail now," I muse.

"I must've gotten on some list. Anyway, if you could take a look at it and then toss it in the recycling bin, that would be a huge help."

I sip my tea, savoring its flowery fruitiness. "You got it."

"Thanks. Oh, and one more thing," she says casually. Too casually.

"Sure, anything."

"Call Rosemary and let her know about the wedding? Kaythanksbye."

I'm mid-spit take, spewing herbal tea, when the phone goes quiet in my ear. I try to be irritated with my baby sister, but her maneuver was so masterful, so well played, that the only emotion I can muster is grudging admiration and respect.

I gaze out at Muffy's garden, in full bloom this time of year, and finish my tea, steeling myself for the call I'm about to make.

CHAPTER 3

Rosemary

I wipe the sweat from the back of my neck with a dishtowel and curse the muggy Los Angeles weather. Back home, I'd be rooting for a good thunderstorm to break the heat and wash away the humidity. But I'm in for a long wait if I think my little corner of Westwood is going to get rain. It's been a hot, dry summer.

As if he can read my mind, Dave flashes me a crooked grin as he climbs out of the back of the catering truck. "It sure is hot. We should get out of town for a few days."

"Yeah," I crack. "I know, let's go to the desert."

We've decided that even though Thyme and

Victor's surprise engagement party is off, we're going to make the trip anyway.

In part, because we've already arranged for a free four-day weekend. And it's no small feat for us to align our schedules this way.

Running my own catering company means my weekends are rarely my own. Parties tend to happen on Friday and Saturday nights. Wednesday morning books are few and far between. I've been trying to expand my corporate lunch business to ease the weekend crunch.

Dave has even less flexibility than I do. Although he has scheduled work shifts, it turns out that people aren't super-obliging about when they die. Homicide detectives like Dave are pretty much on call, well, all the time. But he called in a bunch of favors and agreed to work the next five weekends, so we're going to make the most of this one.

Also, it's too late to cancel the private house we rented in a small community outside Vegas. There's no point losing our deposit. So, we're loading our bags, Mona Lisa's dog bed and collection of squeakies, stuffies, and ropes into the back of the van. I suppose a catering van seems like an odd vehicle choice for a road trip, but it's actually perfect—roomy, air-conditioned throughout, and already stocked with kitchen utensils and pantry basics that will come in handy at the rental house.

Dave brushes his palms against one another. "I think that's it. Except for Mona Lisa."

I hand him her bright purple leash. "Last I saw her, she was sprawled out in the bathtub."

One eyebrow shoots toward his hairline. "Seriously?"

"I think the porcelain or whatever it is must be cool on her belly."

He gives me a skeptical look, but her behavior seems pretty reasonable to me. I'd hate to be a black dog living in Southern California.

"Okay, I'll get her. You pull up the directions?"

I lean over and kiss the side of his neck. "You got it, babe."

He pulls me in and kisses me back.

"Ick, you're all sweaty. " I push him away, jokingly, but not really.

He lifts my hair from my damp neck. "Yeah, and you're … glistening."

"Go get the dog. I'll get the air conditioning running."

He jogs toward the apartment, and I slide into the driver's seat of the van and crank the air conditioning to full blast. I can hear Sage's voice in my mind, calmly informing me that cranking the A/C doesn't cool down the interior of the vehicle any faster.

"Yeah, well, it makes me feel like I'm doing something," I mutter aloud to the voice in my head.

It's probably my biggest flaw. I'm constitutionally incapable of letting things *be.* I have to exert my will and try to fix it, change it, handle it—whatever *it* is.

Intellectually, I know this character trait is probably why Thyme called Sage, and not me, to talk about her heartbreak and, presumably, her breakup with Victor. I know this, but the truth is, it still stings. I want to be there for Thyme, just as much as Sage does.

My stomach tightens at the thought of Thyme, in the middle of nowhere, New Mexico, in the throes of relationship drama. My baby sister.

I hope Sage was able to give her some support.

As if I've summoned her by thinking of her, Sage's name flashes across my cell phone screen as my ringtone sounds.

I fumble with the phone and answer the call.

"Hey, how is she?"

Sage laughs. "Fine. Better than fine, in fact."

"She must be in denial. Poor Thyme." I frown at how dense Sage is being. What she says next turns my frown into an 'O' of surprise.

"No, actually, she's doing great. She and Victor *are* getting married."

"What? They are?"

"Yep. The day after tomorrow. In Vegas. You didn't cancel the house yet, did you?"

I realize my mouth is hanging open and clamp my jaw shut.

"Rosie?"

Oh, right. I have to open it again to speak.

"Sorry, I'm here. No, I didn't cancel the house."

Great! I'll see you tomorrow, right?"

Back when we thought we were going to Las Vegas to celebrate our sister's engagement, we'd agreed to arrive the day before to catch up and hang out. Dave and I are adding one extra day on to the original plan by leaving today.

"Sure, but I don't understand. The wedding's in two days?"

"Right."

"What is she thinking?"

"Here's the thing—the reason she initially told Victor no is she doesn't want a big wedding."

"Okay, but even a small wedding will take us more than forty-eight hours to pull together. I mean, even if we split up the tasks among the six of us, I don't think there's any way ...." I trail off, envisioning a color-coded spreadsheet with target deadlines. I'm going to have to run back inside and grab my laptop.

Then my brain catches up, and I switch gears. "Wait. How does she expect anyone other than us to be able to attend this wedding? Mom and Dad need time to make arrangements. And Victor's parents are in freaking Brazil."

Sage's voice is gentle. "They want a private ceremony and then a nice dinner with us. That's it, Rosemary. No reception, no other family, no friends. They say they'll have a big party later, after Mom and Dad have been released. And I guess they'll go to Brazil and do it again."

"But why?"

A long *whoosh* of air, then she says, "She's convinced something terrible will befall her if she plans a wedding."

"What, like a hoodoo curse?" I can't resist poking at Sage.

"Or, like, being abducted by a loan shark and held hostage in a storage container," she pokes right back.

I shrug. To an outsider, Thyme's conviction that a wedding reception will bring bad luck may sound unhinged. But, frankly? Given our family track record, I can see why she'd want to avoid one. I decide to get on board.

"Okay, but I'm baking them a cake."

"Ro—"

"It's nonnegotiable." I use my big sister voice.

She makes a small sound, as if she's choking back a laugh. "That's fair. I'll let her know to call you if she has any flavor requests."

Dave's headed out of the building, Mona Lisa bounding along beside him.

"I have to run. Have a safe flight, Sage."

"Thanks, see you tomorrow. And, Rosie?"

"Hmm?"

"She's making the right decision for *her.* It might not be the one either of us would make, but—"

"I know. I sure hope it works out the way she's envisioning."

Sage chuckles. "What could possibly go wrong? All she needs to do is get the marriage license."

As I end the call, I tell myself she's right. Still, though, a weird sense of foreboding settles around me.

CHAPTER 4

Thyme

By the time we roll into the Arizona retirement community where Victor's next interviews are scheduled, the orange sun is low in the sky.

"The marketing coordinator said you're welcome to use the community pool or gym while I talk to the Mortensons." Victor parks the rental car in a spot in front of the residential sales office and flashes me a smile.

As I scoop up my messenger bag and step out of

the car, I spare a longing gaze at the brilliant blue water in the deserted Olympic-sized pool.

"It looks so inviting, but I better not. I'm going to boot up my laptop and apply for the marriage license online so we can pick it up in the morning when we get to Las Vegas."

At the mention of marriage, a surprisingly shy expression crosses his face.

"Are you *blushing?*"

He makes a tsking noise. "What? No!"

I twist my lips into a skeptical bow and examine him. "You totally are. Who knew you'd be the blushing groom?"

He wraps an arm around my waist and reels me close. "My secret's out. I'm head over heels for you, Thyme Field."

I stare up into his warm, dark eyes. "Your secret's safe with me," I whisper.

"Only for another day. After that, the whole world will know."

I smile as the excitement in my chest threatens to bubble over. "Go, do your interview." I kiss him hard and send him on his way.

He's only gone about ten feet when a sudden worry pops into my mind.

"Wait!"

He turns back. "What's wrong?"

"I need your driver's license or passport … or I don't know … how do I apply for a marriage license for a naturalized citizen? What if you need additional paperwork? What if—?"

He searches through his laptop bag then strides back and presses his wallet and passport into my hands. "All my papers are in here. It's gonna be fine. I'm sure the Clerk's Office in Clark County, Nevada, of all places, has plenty of experience in issuing marriage licenses under *all sorts* of unusual circumstances. A naturalized citizen isn't going to throw anyone there for a loop."

I take a breath. He's right.

"You're right."

"I know." He winks and walks off.

I take another breath and eye the pool area again. Three minutes later, I'm set up at a wrought-iron table, shaded from the sun by a large canvas umbrella, tapping away on my keyboard with a view of the placid pool. The application, or pre-application, as the website refers to it, is simple enough. I zip through Victor's section, copying the required information from his passport and social security card. Oddly enough, I stumble over my own information.

The form asks if I'm planning to change my name.

Am I?

Thyme Magnolia Field. Thyme Magnolia Callais. Thyme Magnolia Field-Callais. Thyme Field Callais.

It occurs to me that this is my chance. I could type 'Elizabeth Jones' into this form and never hear another crack about my name as long as I live. But, I'm Thyme. I'll always be Thyme. The last name, though, is trickier.

I almost pull my phone out to consult Rosemary, but I stop myself. I'm about to be a married woman. I need to make decisions for myself. I trap my lower lip between my teeth and ponder. I notice that my heart is chugging along like a train, which seems a bit dramatic for filling out a county government form. But, in the immortal words of my dad, it is what it is.

Finally, I type 'Thyme Magnolia Field-Callais.'

I lean back and study the words. Too long. And, let's be real, Thyme is plenty unusual as far as names go, without gilding the magnolia, as it were. Plus the hyphen creates a set of issues all its own.

I backspace. 'Thyme Field Callais.' I narrow my eyes at the screen, then nod. That feels right.

With a sense of enormous relief, I move on.

What's this? Now the form wants to know the 'couple's mailing address'? My heart ratchets up from thudding to about-to-explode-drumbeat.

We've literally never discussed this. This can't be a decision I make alone. Victor and I need to talk.

But I also need to submit this pre-application before the close of business. I pick up my phone and tell the voice assistant to flip a coin. Heads, we'll use Victor's address on the form; tails, mine.

"Heads," the disembodied female voice informs me.

Victor's address is it. I key it into the field, scan the form for errors or omissions, then press submit.

After a moment's celebration, I stand, stretch, and close my eyes, turning my face up to the sky to be warmed by the sun.

I check the time and pack up my laptop, then head into the pool house, bouncing lightly on my toes. With the online marriage application finished, it looks like I'll have time to go for a swim after all.

Everything's falling into place for a quiet wedding to the man who fills my heart. In two short days, I'll be Thyme Field Callais. I giggle to myself as I dig my swimsuit out of my bag.

I feel vibrant, fully alive.

CHAPTER 5

Thyme

"I'm very clearly not dead." I grip the edge of the counter to ground myself to reality as I grind out the words from between my clenched teeth.

The Clark County Clerk of Courts is not impressed. He eyeballs me over his wire-rimmed glasses. "I don't know what to tell you, ma'am. Your name …" He pauses to squint at the printout in his hands. "… Thigh-me Magnolia Field and your social are direct matches with a listing on the Death Index. You died just over three weeks ago," he helpfully informs me.

"Except I'm alive," I say. I really try to tamp down my snark because I need this man's help. But *come on.*

"Which can only mean you aren't Thyme Magnolia Field." He tries to hide the snicker in his voice at my name, but it's there.

I decide to appeal to that ridicule. "Right. Because if I were taking on a fake identity, I'd definitely choose a name like this. Obviously I'm really me."

He's not having it. He's already looking over my shoulder, ready to gesture the next couple forward.

Victor breaks in. "Wait. This Death Index, where did you get it?"

The clerk flips his eyes toward the ceiling but turns and answers the question. "It's the Social Security Death Index. The SSDI is compiled from the Social Security Administration's Master Death File. If your name is in that database, somebody reported you as deceased to the Social Security Administration."

"Does this federal government database ever contain errors?" Victor presses, placing an ever-so-slight emphasis on the words *federal government database* as if to suggest to the clerk that they both know bureaucracies screw up from time to time.

The man snorts and pushes his glasses up to the crown of his head. He looks from side to side, then leans over the counter. "Pal, I really hope your lady friend didn't end up in the MDF by mistake. Because from what I've heard, clearing that up is a Kafkaesque nightmare that'll leave you and her wishing she *were* dead."

With that, he pushes the denial of our marriage pre-application across the counter to us and beckons to the pair of lovebirds behind us.

I scoop up the papers in a daze, and Victor pilots me through the narrow corridor out into the lobby. I slump against the wall and stare down at the printout in disbelief. It's wild to read the words in black and white, but there they are: 'Thyme Magnolia Field, deceased, Snow City, Arizona.'

My date and place of birth are correct, and so is my social security number. But I've never heard of—let alone visited—Snow City, Arizona. And I definitely didn't die there three weeks ago.

I give my head a vigorous shake in an effort to clear my mind. "I can't believe this."

He crooks a finger under my chin and tips my head back. "We'll get it cleared up. You're obviously alive."

"We might not get it straightened out before tomorrow," I warn him.

He shrugs. "My desire to marry you doesn't have an expiration date, Thyme."

I grin at him and resolve not to obsess about the

administrative mix-up. Despite what the clerk says, I'm confident we will get it sorted. It just may take a while.

"Come on," I say. "My sisters should be here by now. If anything will take my mind off being dead, it's hanging out with Rosemary and Sage."

~

I TAKE A TURN BEHIND THE WHEEL WHILE VICTOR navigates. The poor guy did all the driving the past two days—through New Mexico, Arizona, and all the way to Clark County, Nevada.

"Arizona," I say aloud as a question pops into my mind.

"You want to play the alphabet game? Sure. A my name is Arturo and I'm going to Arizona with an automobile full of anteaters."

"What?" I glance away from the road to throw him a puzzled look.

"You must know the alphabet game. Did you ever play it with your sisters on car rides when you were a kid?"

I think back. "No, we mainly came up with spells and chattered in this gibberish fairy language that we made up."

"Oh-kay."

It's basically impossible to explain my childhood, so I don't even try. "Back to Arizona."

"Sure."

"Did we drive near or through Snow City yesterday?"

The retirement community where the Mortensons live is due west of Phoenix, so we drove from there to Las Vegas last night, stopping for dinner at a roadside diner about two hours into our trip. I don't remember seeing signs for Snow City anywhere on our route through Arizona, but seeing as how I supposedly died there, I'm curious about this desert town with snow in its name.

He makes a pinching motion over his cell phone screen and scrutinizes a map. I return my attention to the road.

After a moment he says, "Hmm, no. We took Route 10 to Interstate 93 and came into town from the south. It's supposed to be the more scenic route. But if we'd taken Route 60 to 93, we would have driven right by Snow City on our way into town."

"Really?"

"Really. It looks like it's maybe … a hundred miles from Snow City to The Strip."

"Huh," I say, not sure why I felt the need to place a town that's nothing to me.

He closes out the map app. "Do you want to stop by the hotel and freshen up or go straight to your sisters' rental?"

I check the time on the dashboard clock. "No, let's head out to Cerro Vista. I'm sure we'll probably all have dinner on The Strip, so we can pop into the room then."

I want to get it over with—the part where I tell my sisters that there's probably not going to be a wedding tomorrow because the government thinks I'm a dead woman. A high, hysterical laugh, almost a cackle, bubbles up from deep in my throat. I swallow it as best I can, but I can feel Victor eyeing me.

CHAPTER 6

Sage

I'm checking out the pool in the backyard of the rental with Rosemary and Dave's dog when I hear the sound of a car engine. The vehicle pulls into the driveway on the other side of the tall privacy fence, and the driver kills the engine.

Thyme and Victor have arrived.

"Come on, Mona Lisa." I pat the side of my thigh.

She lopes across the yard toward me, then heels beside me. I push open the sliding glass door and we run through the open, airy first floor of the house, headed for the front door.

"Thyme's here," I call up the spiral staircase as I rush by.

Rosemary is constitutionally incapable of living out of a suitcase, so she's probably up there refolding all her socks and arranging them just so in a dresser drawer.

Dave calls back something indistinct that lets me know they heard me.

I rush out onto the front stoop with Rosemary's dog by my side. Victor smiles and raises his hand in a greeting while Thyme slides out from behind the wheel of the car. We both start running and meet in an artfully arranged rock garden.

I squeak out a hello while she squeezes me tight. As I hug her back, the dog barks. One short bark to let Thyme know she's there. My sister releases me and squats on her heels to pet Mona Lisa.

Victor approaches with a large duffle bag slung over one shoulder and Thyme's messenger bag and his laptop bag over the other.

"Hi, Sage."

"Victor, I'm so happy for you two!" I fling my arms open to invite a brotherly hug.

As we embrace, his eyes meet Thyme's, and a fraught look passes between them.

Fraught probably sounds like a strange way to

describe a glimpse shared by lovers who are about to become newlyweds, but I swear it's the right word. The exchange is loaded with emotion, but none of it's good. Instead of love and affection, I sense anxiety and tension.

I pull back and examine the two of them. "What's wrong?"

Another sidelong glance bounces from Thyme to Victor.

"Nothing," she says airily. Too airily. She waves a hand toward the driveway. "Did Rosemary really drive out here in her catering truck?"

It's an obvious gambit, designed to distract me from ... whatever's causing the friction between them. But I go along with it.

"She says it's more comfortable for the dog than riding in her car. And, besides, there's a mobile kitchen pantry in the back in case she has trouble sourcing any of the ingredients for your cake."

I smile, but Thyme doesn't. Her lips are drawn and her forehead is furrowed.

"What cake?"

My eyes flit from her face to Victor's and then back to hers before I answer.

"She understands you don't want any sort of reception tomorrow, but she's hoping you'll let her make you a cake. It would mean a lot to her Thyme. She made her own cake, and mine. She wants to complete the circle and give you the cake of your heart." I pause and frown. "Those are her words, not mine. 'Cake of your heart.' I feel like it should be 'cake of your gut,' but I guess that lacks a certain flair, huh?"

I snicker at my own joke, but they're both straight-faced and silent.

"Oh, come on. It's bad manners to leave me hanging like this. At least fake a polite chuckle. Jeez."

Still nothing.

"What's wrong?" I repeat.

Victor sighs. "Let's take this stuff inside. We'll tell all four of you about it."

I can't read Thyme's expression, which is unusual for me. She's my baby sister, after all. I've had a lifetime of practice interpreting her emotions. Maybe she's rethinking the whole 'no reception' idea.

"Sure," I chirp. "Dave mentioned something about mixing up a pitcher of margaritas, if you're interested."

"Sounds great," Thyme says flatly as I lead her and Victor into the house.

"Wow, nice place," Victor says, taking in the open floor plan, the wide windows that showcase the mountain view, and the clean, white lines.

"It is, isn't it?" Rosemary calls from the vast marble

kitchen island, where she's chopping vegetables. Dave's beside her, at work on the promised drinks.

She wipes her hands on her cute striped apron and hurries into the entryway to envelope first Thyme, then Victor, in a hug.

Dave waves hello from the kitchen, which makes me realize I haven't seen Roman in a while.

As if on cue, he comes walking into the kitchen from the attached garage with an armload of wood.

"Hey, you're here," he exclaims, nodding his head in greeting to my sister and her fiancé. "Check it out—there's a big pile of wood in the garage. I thought I'd get the fire pit all set up so we can have a fire tonight."

"Sounds great," Dave tells him, abandoning his bartender duties to slide open the door to the back-yard for Roman.

Roman loves fire. Not in an arsonist kind of way. In a bonfires on the beach, flames in the fireplace, candles scattered around the house kind of way. Even money says he returns to Hilton Head Island with plans to erect a fire pit or outdoor fireplace some-where on Chip and Muffy's property, where we're still living in the guest cottage.

Thinking about our living arrangement reminds me.

"Hey, where are you two going to live after you get

married?" I say to Thyme. "Are you keeping your place or Victor's?"

I've never seen Victor's apartment, but I hope it's bigger than Thyme's cramped one-bedroom. Although, to be fair, calling it a one-bedroom is a bit of an exaggeration. Her 'bedroom' is roughly the size of a utility closet.

Another tense look passes between Victor and Thyme.

Rosemary notices. "Uh-oh. Can't decide?"

"No. It's not that—" Thyme begins.

In that moment, Roman returns from the backyard and Dave announces that it's margarita time. I grit my teeth and trail the others out into the loggia, which is glassed in on three sides and looks out over the pool. Despite the midday heat, the space is airy and comfortable, thanks, no doubt, to the set of large paddle fans lazily circling on the ceiling above.

We settle into seats. The outdoor furniture is all teak wood and tasteful cushions, like something out of a movie or a catalogue for a store even Muffy and Chip couldn't afford. I hope I don't spill my drink on the fabric.

Mona Lisa is evidently less intimidated than I am. She waits for Rosemary to sit back, then springs up onto her lap, knocking her tail against Rosemary's glass in her enthusiasm.

Dave finishes passing out the margaritas and raises his glass. "To Thyme and Victor, may tomorrow be the start of a long and happy life together, full of love and laughter."

Rosemary clinks her glass against his, and we all toast Thyme and Victor.

Thyme smiles weakly and sips her drink. Then she clears her throat.

"So, yeah, about tomorrow. The clerk's office denied our wedding license application."

"What?" I sputter and narrowly avoid doing a spit take. Roman thumps me on the back.

"Because of Victor's citizenship?" Dave guesses.

"Nope," Victor says. "Because of Thyme's ... uh, death."

"Pardon?" Rosemary blinks at him.

"Yeah, so, somehow the Social Security Administration got the idea that I'm deceased." Thyme fakes a laugh, but her heart's not in it.

I squint at her, trying to make sense of what she's saying.

"So, they have you mixed up with someone else. Shouldn't that be an easy mistake to correct?" Roman asks.

"Apparently, it's not. The guy at the clerk's office told us that getting off the Death Index is some extra-special layer of bureaucratic hell."

Dave nods, knowingly. "The Social Security Administration's death files make up the authoritative database of deaths in the U.S. Once your name is added to the master file, you're officially dead for all intents and purposes."

He's a homicide detective, so I imagine he's had more experience with death files than the rest of us have.

"All intents and purposes, including getting married," Thyme says mournfully. She drains her margarita glass and gestures for Dave to refill it from the pitcher.

I open my mouth to caution her, but Roman catches my eye and gives me a wordless warning. I guess he's right—who am I to tell a dead woman how much she should drink?

"Um, so … did the clerk give you any details about your … death?" I ask instead.

"Let's see. It happened twenty-two days ago in a town called Snow City, Arizona." She shrugs.

"Cause of death?" Rosemary asks.

Thyme shakes her head no. Victor cracks, "Administrative incompetence would be my guess."

Everyone roars with laughter, except Thyme. I can tell by her wobbly bottom lip that she's trying not to cry. I put down my glass to go comfort her, but Victor beats me to it.

As he caresses her shoulder, Rosemary catches my eye and jerks her head toward the kitchen. I follow her back inside, leaving Roman and Dave to make small talk with the walking dead and her fiancé.

CHAPTER 7

Rosemary

I pull Sage into the kitchen and close the door to the loggia behind her.

"What's the big emergency?"

"We have to do something."

She looks at me blankly.

"To help Thyme," I elaborate. "So she can get married."

"It's ludicrous that she's been declared dead, for sure—but what do you have in mind? How can we possibly fix this?"

She's looking at me expectantly, and I realize the

question isn't rhetorical. I don't have an answer. I just know we need to *do* something. If there's one thing I hate, it's not having the answer. It's either one of my greatest strengths or one of my biggest weaknesses. Possibly both.

I rack my brain, searching for an answer. She folds her arms over her chest and watches me. It's hard to think when someone's staring at you.

My face flames under her scrutiny. I can't believe I'm blushing. To top it off, the heat rising off my skin makes me wish we were having this conversation on a snowy mountaintop, rather than in the sweltering Mojave desert.

Inspiration smacks me in the sweaty noggin.

"We have to go there."

"Go where?"

"Snow City. We need to go to Arizona and poke around. Somebody died there. It just wasn't Thyme."

She scrunches up her nose but says nothing.

"What?" I prod her.

"It's not a *bad* idea, but . . . if this is all because someone transposed a number in a social security number or something, showing up in the town where the woman died isn't going to change anything. If that's what happened, Thyme simply needs to file some paperwork with the SSA to get it corrected."

She eyeballs me as if she's daring me to argue.

I don't. Instead I counter, "Once an accountant, always an accountant."

"What does that even mean?"

I exhale slowly. "It means maybe you're right. Maybe all Thyme needs to do is complete Form Whatever in triplicate, get it notarized, submit it, and wait three months. But even if that's true, it's not helpful right now. We can't let her sit around, suck down margaritas, and mope. She thought she was going to get married tomorrow. If that's not going to happen, we should keep her busy to keep her mind off it."

I watch Sage's posture soften as she considers what I'm saying.

Finally, she nods. "I guess you're right. If nothing else, a road trip will be a distraction. But, man, I kind of like this house. It's a shame to leave a great place with a pool right on the outskirts of Las Vegas to go traipsing off to Icetown, Arizona or wherever."

"Snow City," I correct her automatically.

She blinks, then her eyes go wide. She tears out of the kitchen and races up the staircase to the second floor.

Roman turns his head and gives me a *'what's she up to?'* look through the glass wall, and I shrug. I don't have the faintest idea.

I hear her banging around in the bedroom she and Roman claimed as theirs. A hot minute later, she's back. She jogs down the stairs carrying tall stacks of rubber-banded mail in both hands.

"Come on," she pants at me as she zips through the kitchen on her way back outside.

My curiosity piqued, I follow her.

She dumps the piles of mail on the glass-topped table and starts riffling through the envelopes with both hands.

"What are you looking for?" Dave asks, strolling over from the pool with his margarita in hand to watch her frantic search.

"Thyme's doorman had a bunch of her mail delivered to my place yesterday. Apparently, her box has filled up while she's been on the road with Victor."

Victor nods. "I'm surprised she got so much. Usually, neither of us gets any regular mail. Everything comes electronically."

Sage twists around to look at him. "This is maybe a tenth of what Doolittle forwarded to me. You wouldn't believe all the magazines and catalogs Thyme gets."

Thyme, who's been staring off into space, jolts to attention. "What? No, I don't get junk mail. I had my name taken off all those lists years ago. Do you know how wasteful those mailers are? Not just the paper used, but also the energy consumed in printing them and delivering them. He must've given you someone else's mail."

"No, it was definitely yours. All sorts of stuff that you wouldn't ordinarily be interested in, but the mailers had your name on them. I specifically checked."

I ping-pong my head back and forth between the two of them like I'm watching a tennis match.

Thyme frowns. "Like what sort of stuff?"

Sage gnaws on her lip as she tries to remember. "Um, fancy French cookware, a bunch of essential oils and natural cleaning products—"

"Well, that second one doesn't sound totally out of character. The first one, yeah—assuming Thyme is still using her oven as sweater storage."

"She is," Victor assures me.

I shake my head.

Sage continues as if we haven't interrupted, "—boutique baby clothes, custom-made purses, makeup."

Thyme's expression is blank. "I don't know why I would've gotten that stuff. Did you pitch it?"

"Yeah, the advertisements and all the credit card offers went straight into the recycling bin. But I did keep anything that looked like real mail, and there's a lot of that, too—clearly."

She falls silent.

Thyme returns her attention to her drink.

We all watch Sage continue to paw through the small mound of mail like a manic squirrel desperately seeking a nut.

"Yeah!" she shouts in triumph, waving around a business-size envelope.

"What is it?" I crane my head to get a better view of the utterly normal-looking piece of mail.

"It's a letter from a dentist's office addressed to Thyme."

To say this announcement is anticlimactic doesn't do justice to our collective groans and crestfallen expressions.

"Dr. Rubin's office? It's probably a reminder that I'm due for a cleaning."

"No!" Sage practically shouts, gesticulating wildly. "It's from Dr. Alexis Pridemore in Snow City, Arizona."

Thyme lunges for the envelope and rips it open. I hold my breath while she scans the letter inside.

"Well?" Victor demands.

She raises her head. "Dr. Pridemore wanted to let me know my new dentures are ready to be fitted."

CHAPTER 8

Thyme

We're all piled into Rosemary's catering truck, barreling along the highway toward the Arizona border. Rosemary's driving and, somehow, Sage scored the shotgun seat.

Dave, Victor, Roman, Mona Lisa, and I are wedged shoulder to shoulder to tail to shoulder along the wall opposite the small prep sink and dorm fridge, which appear to be securely affixed to the side of the truck. I hope so, at least.

Beside me, the dog has her snout lowered to the bottom of her dog bed and her paws crossed over her eyes. She swishes her tail hard against my thigh, and I get the impression she wants me to know she's put out at having to share her space with four loud, clumsy humans.

At least you've got a nice soft bed, I think, as I shift on my sit bones in a fruitless effort to find a more comfortable position.

I give up and elbow Dave. "How did Sage manage to claim the passenger seat?"

He gives me a wry smile. "Age-old tradition. She shouted 'shotgun' as she ran from the house to the driveway."

Sage looks in the rearview mirror and raises her hand in a triumphant fist pump. I roll my eyes but can't stop myself from giggling.

"Are you feeling the effects of two margaritas in the space of ten minutes?" Victor asks in a low, concerned voice.

"No," I assure him. "Feeling the effects of being on this mission with my sisters and my three favorite guys."

Mona Lisa huffs.

"And the world's best doggo," I add.

A slow smile spreads across Victor's face. It starts at his full lips, but it doesn't stop there. His cheeks curve upward, and his eyelids relax. For the first time since we found out I'm, you know, dead, his expression is fully relaxed. I realize this mess has been bothering him almost as much as it's been stressing me out. I reach for his hand and give it a squeeze.

He raises my hand to his lips and brushes the back of it with a soft kiss.

Roman makes a gagging sound. "Get a room, already."

I shoot him a caustic look, and he dissolves into peals of laughter. "Kidding," he gasps.

The silly mood inside the van is infectious. Part of it—maybe most of it—is the relief of having something tangible we can do to try to prove that I'm not a dead, denture-wearing woman from Snow City, Arizona. And, as Dave the detective quickly pointed out, dental records will go a long way to showing that the dead woman, whoever she is, isn't me. So, I'm giving this trip a high likelihood of success.

The other reason for our group goofiness is that we're on a mission. We've done this sort of thing before. After all, Rosemary, Sage, and I did all fall in love with these men after investigating crimes with them. And, on two occasions, we've all teamed up to solve a mystery.

I gasp.

"What?" The playfulness vanishes from Victor's eyes in an instant, replaced by a wary alertness.

Dave and Roman both also turn their heads at the sound of my sharp intake of breath.

Oops.

"Sorry, guys, I didn't mean to startle you. It just hit me that the whole reason I wanted to elope was to avoid the part of the wedding preparations where the six of us are trying to solve a mystery. Best-laid plans, I guess."

Victor relaxes, and the others laugh softly.

Dave leans forward. "Thyme, I think you're going to have to come to grips with the indelible fact that you and your sisters have a genetic predisposition to hijinks, for lack of a better word."

Roman nods in eager agreement. "I mean, it's clearly hereditary. Look at your parents."

It's hard to refute his point seeing as how both my parents currently reside in federal prisons. At least my sisters and I generally stay on the right side of the law during our escapades. I mean, more or less. At least, when it's practical to do so.

I'm about to point out this helpful fact, but Sage takes a different tack. She whips her head around, her red curls bouncing as she turns to face her husband, jabbing her finger in the air.

"One, I heard that. And, two, you're one to talk, what with your meddling mom, sneaky aunt, and criminal stepsister."

Zing.

Sage smiles warmly to soften the sting, but she's got a point. She may have gone off on a literal ghost chase before her wedding, but it *was* all Roman's family's doing. Roman's sheepish grin suggests that he doesn't disagree.

The fact that Sage can place her chaotic wedding at the feet of the Lyman family is in stark contrast to what happened at Rosemary and Dave's wedding. Their wedding drama was one hundred percent caused by our side of the family—specifically Mom and Dad, who at that point in time were fugitives from the law, and the sleazy, mobbed-up loan shark they got mixed up with.

But this time, neither the Callais family nor, thank heavens, the Field family is responsible for the federal government deciding that I'm a dead woman . . . at least, not as far as I know. I narrow my eyes and study my fellow travelers as if I might uncover a mistake one of them made. Nah, nobody in this crowded catering van's to blame.

The question remains: who *is?*

Mona Lisa raises her head and gives me an indecipherable look. I guess she doesn't know either. But with any luck, a quick trip to Snow City will answer all my questions—and maybe, just maybe, by this time tomorrow, Victor and I will be standing in front of an officiant.

I close my eyes and lean into his side, and he drapes his arm around me as the van bounces along the highway.

~

THE TRIP FROM CERRO VISTA TO THE CENTER OF SNOW City takes ninety minutes, exactly. Rosemary pulls the van into a public parking lot, and we tumble out of the back, stretching and yawning—and, in one case, peeing on a bush.

"Good girl," Rosemary says to the dog as she exits the van and feeds a handful of quarters into the meter.

"Now what?" Sage wants to know.

Rosemary points at a squat white building across the street. "Thyme's dentist's office is in there. She should go see what she can find out from Doctor Pridemore while we check out the town."

"That's fair," I say. I hardly need an entourage of five plus one canine to talk to a dentist. "Do you want to come with me?" I direct the question to Victor.

He's busy looking around. When he turns toward me, a faint frown creases his mouth. "Sure, if you're looking for company."

I am, or at least I was. But now I'm more interested in what's caught his attention. "Is something wrong?"

"Don't you notice what's missing?"

I scan the parking lot. "A sign that says we can pay for parking through an app?"

"It's the people," Dave pipes up. "Where are all the people?"

"Bingo," Victor says.

We all turn our heads from side to side in unison. We look like a pack of cats tracking a mouse—or a laser toy. Victor and Dave are right. The town square is strangely deserted.

"Maybe they're all at work and school?" Sage offers.

"It's one o'clock in the afternoon," Rosemary points out. "Shouldn't someone be out grabbing lunch or running errands?"

I study the row of glass-fronted buildings that sit on the other side of a small alley running behind the parking lot. None of them appear to be businesses. At least none of them have any signage that suggests retail activity happens within them.

"There must be a mall on the outskirts of town."

"A mall? What, is it 1986 here? The people of Snow City probably do their shopping like the rest of America—online, one-click, free delivery or in-store pickup, which they'll swing by and take care of on their way home from work," I tell them.

My sisters shrug wordlessly at one another: this is older sibling code for *yeah, she's right, but we'll never admit it.*

That's okay, though. I know what the gesture means as well as they do, and I file away my silent victory with a small smile.

Roman rubs his hands over his forearms as if he's warding off a chill. "Still. It's creepy. Not a single car has passed by while we've been standing here . . . on Main Street, no less."

Victor nods his agreement. "Maybe this is one of those Western ghost towns people talk about."

"There are ghost towns around here?" Sage looks over her shoulder.

I resist the urge to shout *'Boo!,'* but barely.

"They're not haunted, just abandoned. You know, deserted mining towns and stuff." Rosemary gives her a look of disbelief.

Sage grimaces, and I instantly feel about an inch tall. After all, she did go through a period right before her wedding when someone tried to make her believe she was cursed by an angry spirit. Apparently, she isn't entirely over the experience yet.

Rosemary also catches Sage's reaction and nudges her shoulder. "Come on, while Thyme subjects herself to the dentist, let's see if we can find a candy shop or an ice cream parlor in this town."

"Oh—or a bakery," Dave chimes in. "I could go for a donut."

I consider making a donut-loving cop joke, but I'm not one to go after the low-hanging fruit. Instead, I shake my head. "Listen to you. You all should be seeing the dentist, not me. You're going to give yourself cavities as you eat through this town's supply of sugary treats."

My sisters groan.

"Where should we meet back up with you?" Victor wants to know.

Rosemary scans both sides of the street, then points to a small park dotted with cacti, boulders, and benches. "We won't roam too far. After we ruin our teeth, we'll be in that park playing with Mona Lisa."

At the sound of her name, Mona Lisa barks approvingly.

I turn to Victor. "You ready?"

"Let's do this."

We walk toward the building that houses the dental office.

"Good luck," Sage calls after us.

I acknowledge her with a wave over my shoulder, then I slip my hand inside Victor's.

He gives it a gentle squeeze. "We've got this."

He sounds so confident. That makes one of us.

CHAPTER 9

Sage

We watch Thyme and Victor stroll across the parking lot. Once they disappear into the lobby of the white building, I turn to Rosemary.

"We're not really getting sweets, right?"

She gives me a long, cool look. "No. I thought we might try to find a wedding gift from the four of us—just in case a miracle happens and they can go forward with the ceremony tomorrow."

"That's great! I had the same idea," I chirp.

"Did you?" Her tone is as chilly as her expression.

"Yeah, I did. What's your deal, anyway?" I shoot back.

Over her shoulder, I see Dave and Roman exchanging panicked looks. Dave bobs his head. "I think Mona Lisa needs to do her business. Come on, Roman, let's stretch our legs."

Rosemary twists around to face them. Her husband gives her a warm smile. "After you and your sister sort out the, uh, gift, come over to the park."

He starts walking before she can object, and Roman throws me a sheepish shrug and trots off after him.

Cowards.

Rosemary turns back to me. "My *deal* is that I know you too well, Sage. I know what you're really up to."

"You do? Then why don't you enlighten me?" As far as I know, I'm not *up to* anything, despite my eldest sister's frosty demeanor.

She sighs deeply and twists her mouth into a little bow of disapproval but doesn't elaborate.

Two can play this game. Well, the *two of us* can. Thyme cannot. She surrenders at the slightest hint of confrontation, unwilling or unable to stand the thought of being in conflict with either of her sisters.

I fold my arms over my chest and cock my head to the side. I wait.

She arches her eyebrows. She waits.

After a thousand years—or maybe a minute and a half—my left cheek starts to itch. I try to ignore it, but the more I focus on not focusing on it, the itchier it becomes. I dig my fingernails into my palms, which somehow makes the itchiness in my face intensify. How is this even scientifically possible?

I could ask my sister, the former scientist, but that would mean speaking first. So I stare at her and will myself not to rake my fingers across my face. I'm not sure why I decide not scratching has to be part of this battle of the wills, but I'm rolling with it now. Even if it feels as if fire ants have taken up residence on my face.

Finally, *finally,* Rosemary breaks the silence.

"Promise me you aren't scheming to get in touch with Mom and Dad," she says, lowering her chin and fixing her eyes on me like lasers.

"Argh, ahhh," I answer, maniacally scoring my fingernails across the side of my face. "Oooh, yeah ...."

"Take your time; I'll wait."

"Sorry, had to scratch an itch. But to answer your question, no, I'm not 'scheming.' I *am* offended, though." I draw myself up and square my shoulders.

She laughs. "You're kidding, right?"

I'm not, and I'm sort of confused as to why she'd think I am. Then it hits me. Like, hits me, physically, as if she punched me in the gut. *Ooof.*

"This is about what happened at your wedding, isn't it?"

"Yes, Sage. Going behind my back and secretly inviting our parents to my wedding caused a lot of problems. You remember, right?"

I exhale, letting go of my urge to defend myself along with my breath, and face her squarely, my palms up and open in a gesture of reaching out.

"I do remember. And I'm sincerely sorry. I hope you know that. And I hope you know I meant well—I thought you'd regret it someday if you looked back at your wedding day and Mom and Dad weren't there."

I still think this, but there's no way I'm going to tell her that in her current mood.

Her face softens, but only for a moment. Then she arches a brow. "Do you think I'll look back with regret on my wedding day and recall that Mom and Dad *were* there and got arrested?"

"I don't know, Rosie. Honestly? I think it's for the best that they've faced the music and are doing their time. Don't you?"

She nods reluctantly. "I do, actually. And I'm glad

they worked it out so they could get day passes to be at your wedding." She pauses meaningfully, then says, "Because I know it really mattered to *you*. But you can't impose your feelings on Thyme. Understand? She's said she'll have a party after they're released. Don't sneak off this afternoon to call and tell them she's eloping. Just ... don't meddle, okay?"

I blink at her. When I answer her, I speak slowly. "I have no intention of trying to get in touch with Mom or Dad this afternoon to fill them in on Thyme's plans."

"Good."

"Besides, you know as well as I do, that we have to go through the proper channels with the Bureau of Prisons to set up a call. I can't just steal away and make a quick call while you're looking at china patterns or something."

"First of all, like we'd buy Thyme and Victor *china.* Second of all, that's a fair point. I'm sorry for being so cranky and distrustful. I know you want our family to be close—or at least less dysfunctional. And, believe it or not, I want that, too. But you have to let me and Thyme manage our own relationships with Mom and Dad."

She manages a smile, but it's a bit wobbly, and her eyes fill. I throw my arms around her.

We hug for a long moment. Then she pulls back and wipes at her eyes with the sleeve of her sweater.

"Come on, let's go shopping."

"Sounds like a plan." I infuse my voice with cheer to match her perky tone.

I meant it when I told her I had no intention of getting in touch with our parents today. I don't plan to call them. I don't need to.

I took care of that yesterday before I left Hilton Head Island.

CHAPTER 10

Thyme

Doctor Pridemore's office is unlike any dentist's office I've ever visited. In my experience, dental practices tend to the sparse and utilitarian, making no pretense at dressing up what they are or what they do. Beige walls, hung with posters showing the anatomy of the tooth—or, if the decorator was really inspired, nature prints. The waiting rooms are cramped and noisy, with wall-mounted televisions blaring daytime talk shows or, worse, cable news. And the magazine selection is nearly always ... vintage.

I've encountered two exceptions to this rule, both, oddly enough, on Hilton Head Island, where Sage lives.

Once, during a visit, she was taking Muffy and Chip's kids to the pediatric dentist and I tagged along. The place looked like what would happen if a LEGO factory and a rainbow had a baby, which was then adopted by a video game company. Bright splashes of primary color everywhere, seating that looked as if it had been constructed out of plastic bricks, and tablets, gaming consoles, and handheld games scattered around the various play zones.

The other time, after we had lunch together in town, Sage popped into the dental studio frequented by the adult Moores to pick up Muffy's forty-dollar charcoal toothpaste (don't ask). That office screamed 'spa.' The waiting lounge was painted in soothing sea foam greens and sky blues, soothing sitar music played softly, pink Himalayan salt rocks and fragrant earthy-smelling oils were placed strategically around the space, and a fancy tea and coffee bar ran along one wall. While Sage acquired the toothpaste, I sank into a plush chair and imagined I lived a life in which a dentist's appointment doubled as a mini-vacation.

But this place—in an ordinary commercial building in the heart of a flyspeck of a town—is in a class of its own. One of a kind. I'm not even sure I can describe it. Judging by the way Victor's gaping as he turns in a slow circle, he's having a similar reaction.

The space itself is ordinary enough. Pale yellow paint on the walls, cream-colored chairs, the ubiquitous TV on the wall. There's a long counter and a receptionist seated behind it.

But across from the reception desk, there's a second counter with glass shelves fronting it. Behind this counter are wall-to-ceiling shelves. It reminds me of an arcade alley prize display—a lot, actually. Only instead of stuffed animals, cheap plastic toys, temporary tattoos, and gold-plated jewelry, this case contains a dizzying assortment of ... stuff. Patterned leggings, quilted purses, natural cleaning supplies from brands I don't recognize, and colorful kitchen implements. On the wall behind the counter, in the place of honor normally reserved for the largest stuffed animals, knock-off iPhones, and remote-controlled drones, there are rows and rows of shelves holding essential oils, makeup palettes, and chunky, gemstone-studded jewelry, as well as face creams, lotions, and potions in sleek, high-end packaging. The only item remotely related to dentistry is a charcoal toothpaste kit with an electronic toothbrush. I recognize it as the same brand Muffy gets on subscription through her dental spa.

"What in the world?" I mutter out of the side of my mouth.

"Duuuude," Victor breathes, every bit as baffled as I am.

We're still standing frozen, staring transfixed at the array of merchandise when the receptionist ends her phone call and trills, "May I help you?"

The waiting room is otherwise empty, so she must be talking to us. I turn, clutching the letter that was delivered to my apartment in New York, and walk forward toward the counter. Victor falls into step beside me. The receptionist watches us with a friendly expression, but her bright green eyes hold a shadow of confusion.

"I hope so," I say as I place the letter down on the counter in front of her. "I got this letter from Doctor Pridemore, but there must be some mistake."

She reaches for the sheet of paper, and as she scans it, I can't help noticing her perfect manicure. Her fingernails are expertly shaped and painted a glossy lilac color.

"I love your nails."

She glances up from the letter, surprise and pleasure lighting her face. "Thanks. I use the Nailtique line."

"I've never heard of it," I confess.

I use whichever bottle catches my eye in the pharmacy, unless it's a special occasion—in which case I put myself in the hands of a professional and let her choose the color. That reminds me. If this wedding is happening tomorrow, I should find a salon in Vegas and book manicure appointments for Sage, Rosemary, and me. My ragged cuticles don't exactly say 'bride.'

"Oh, it's a private line. The entire nail care system is sold through consultants only." Her eyes flit toward the prize case and she points her chin toward the display. "Although I think Dr. Pridemore has a few bottles of the polish over there. And maybe the cuticle oil."

I glance over my shoulder, more baffled than ever, while she returns her attention to the letter.

"Hmm, how did you get this? This address is wrong."

She seems to be talking to herself more than to me, but I respond anyway. "Well, that's my address in New York."

"Yes, but how on earth did Ms. Field's mail end up in New York City? Rest her soul."

Victor leans forward and points. "The date on the letter is six days after Ms. Field died."

It's jarring to hear him talk about me as if I'm dead. I mean, I know he's not talking about me, but still, I'm unsettled by it.

He bumps his leg up against mine, out of the receptionist's sight, as if he can sense the chill that rippled through me.

"I see that. And you think that's important?"

"I wonder if your patient database is somehow connected to the Social Security Administration's, um, master death file and it updated the address automatically to Thyme's address."

"Thyme's address?" she echoes, bewildered.

He shoots me an apologetic look, but I shrug. It was going to have to come out sometime.

"My name is also Thyme Field," I tell her.

"It is? What a coincidence …." She trails off and squints at me.

In a burst of inspiration, I soften my voice and reach for a lie. "Not really. She was my grandmother. I was named for her."

I expect murmured sympathy. At a minimum, a sad smile. Instead, she stiffens.

"Is that so?" She reaches for the intercom without moving her head, keeping her eyes locked on my face, and jabs at a button. "Doctor Pridemore, we have a situation. There's a pair of con artists out here. The woman's impersonating Thyme Field's granddaughter. Do you want to talk to them before I call the sheriff?"

After a long pause, during which I can feel my heart hammering against my chest, a woman's voice crackles through the speaker. "Show them into the consultation room. Bring your pistol."

Con artists? Sheriff? Pistol?!

I wheel around to stare at Victor, whose ashen face doesn't make me feel a bit better. 'Sorry,' I mouth.

CHAPTER 11

Rosemary

As we meander up Snow City's Main Street, Dave and I lag several yards behind Sage and Roman thanks to Mona Lisa's extreme interest in every cactus, succulent, flower, and weed. She homes in on a large spiky agave plant and screeches to a halt to sniff every bushy leaf. I come to a sudden stop, and Dave bumps against the side of my hip.

"Sorry."

"It's okay."

He peers at me, and a vee of concern creases his forehead. "That's it? No smart remark?"

"Oh, uh, watch it, Drummond. You're lucky I don't cite you for a moving violation."

The vee deepens. "That weak sauce is the best you've got? Now I know something's wrong. Talk to me, Rosie."

An involuntary laugh bubbles up in my throat. "My apologies for the weakness of my sauce. I'm distracted."

Mona Lisa decides to further her exploration by tasting her environment.

"Acht." I make the harsh, abbreviated sneeze noise that our dog trainer taught me. To my amazement, she removes her mouth from the prickly plant and eyes me.

"Good girl!" I scritch the special spot behind her ears to reward her for listening.

"Good dog," Dave chimes in. She thumps her tail in response, and we start moving again.

Sage twists over her shoulder to make sure we're still behind her and Roman. I give her a little wave. She flashes a smile.

"Hmm. Did her smile look . . . I don't know . . . tight to you?"

"Tight?"

"Yeah, tight. Thin? Strained?"

"So this distraction, maybe it's guilt?"

He reaches out and places two fingers on my inner wrist, lightly curling his hand around the loop of Mona Lisa's leash. His touch is warmth; it's home; it's comfort. My shoulders ease and my chest expands.

"Maybe. I was pretty hard on her."

"Hmm."

We walk in silence until the dog pauses at a hedgerow.

"But she does have a terrible meddling habit."

"Mm-hmm. She does," he agrees. Then, "Of course, she's always operating from a place of love. Even—no, especially—when she's at her most meddlesome."

"I know," I sigh. It's this truth that's sitting heavy in my throat.

Sage always means well. But that doesn't make the resultant destruction any less messy. Still, though, maybe I was too sharp with her.

Dave chuckles.

"What's so funny?"

"It's not funny, exactly. You and your sisters, you're all so protective of each other. You're trying to protect Thyme from Sage's meddling. The reason Sage invited your parents to our wedding behind your back was to protect you from your ... certainty." He catches himself, substituting in 'certainty' for 'stubbornness,' but his message comes through.

"I suppose you—"

Sage and Roman have reversed course and are striding straight toward us, like race walkers or something.

"Uh-oh. That looks intense."

"Come on, Mona Lisa." I urge her forward, and the three of us start walking—not quite at Sage and Roman's pace, but faster than our regular shambling speed.

Sage is gesturing wildly, urging us to hurry, so I break into a jog. Beside me, Dave does the same.

"What's the matter?" I pant when we reach them.

Maybe Thyme's called, and the meeting with the dentist went poorly.

"This town is weird," she informs me, also slightly out of breath.

"We've already established that."

She gives her curly red hair a shake. "No, really weird."

I cut my eyes to Roman. "You want to translate your wife's gibberish for us?"

"Have you been looking into any of the storefront windows as you walk?" he replies.

"No. Mainly, I've been noticing the bushes. One of the perks of dog ownership."

Sage grabs my arm and yanks me toward the

nearest shop. It appears to be a kitchen goods store. I pass Mona Lisa's leash to Dave as she pulls me past him.

"Look."

"I doubt I'm going to be impressed by their inventory, Sage. I use commercial-quality appliances and accessories, you know."

"Just look," she insists.

I peer through the window at the display. The items are heavy on single-use gadgets in cheerful colors. Tented cards in front of the accessories spell out their names and uses: a bright yellow banana slicer (I use a knife); a vivid green avocado slicer (um, same); and a deep red strawberry huller (seriously, have these people ever heard of a knife?).

I've seen enough. "Okay, this stuff is wholly unnecessary. Anyone with even a modicum of knife skills doesn't need any of it. So?"

She shakes her head. "Notice anything else?"

I return my attention to the window. "It looks like that enamel cooking set in the right corner is a cheap knockoff of the fancy French stuff, but that's not a crime or anything."

"Look at the prices, Rosemary."

I squint at the cards, expecting to see high markups, which, again, wouldn't be surprising. But there are no prices. Not in U.S. dollars at least. The huller, for example, costs 'three snowflakes OBO.' The banana slicer goes for 'four snowflakes, can bundle with two other items for ten snowflakes.' Under each 'price,' what appears to be a street address is printed. All of the knife wannabes have *16 Frost Court* listed.

"Okay, that's weird. But maybe it's just a corny chamber of commerce program, you know, to tie into the town's name."

"All the stores are like this. The products don't have prices, and I don't think they're actually for sale inside," she explains.

"Why would you say that?"

Dave and Roman join us at the window. Roman points toward the counter. "Because there's no cash register."

"They could do electronic transactions, only," Dave suggests. "I think I heard a radio program about it. Some places, maybe in Asia or Europe, are moving in that direction.

"Sure, but credit card companies or bitcoin miners or whatever don't use 'snowflakes' as a unit of currency. And what's with the addresses?" Sage insists.

My stomach grumbles. "Well, there's an easy way to find out. Let's go inside. Maybe they sell snacks, too."

"I'll stay out here with Mona Lisa," Dave offers. "But if they do have any food, grab me a protein bar or some nuts or something, okay?"

"Why don't we walk a little further while they do their recon?" Roman suggests. "There's gotta be a deli or something around here. I'm gonna need more than a package of nuts."

He's a man after my own heart. I could use a bowl of soup and a salad. Or a sandwich. Not a protein bar.

"Sounds like a plan. We'll catch up with you."

Sage's expression is uneasy, so I smile reassuringly at her before I push open the door and drag her inside.

CHAPTER 12

Thyme

So, this is a bad situation. Victor and I are sitting side by side at a small, round table in a slightly less-small square room. The receptionist is standing on the other side of the table, pointing a gun more or less at a spot between my right shoulder and Victor's left. He and I are holding hands under the table, and mine is damp with sweat.

As unnerving as this is—and, believe me, it's extremely unnerving to be looking at the business end of a firearm—I *am* heartened to see that the receptionists' hands are steady and, as far as I can tell, dry.

That's one bright spot. If she shoots one of us, it's likely to be on purpose and not the result of accidentally firing or panicking or something.

Maybe that's not a bright spot so much as a slightly less grim spot. But, I focus on it anyway.

I'm about to ask her what her name is, in part to break the silence and in part so I can attach a name to the person holding us at gunpoint. But as I open my mouth to form the question, the door swings open.

The receptionist flattens herself against the wall to make room for Alexis Pridemore, D.D.S., who squeezes past her and takes the seat across from us.

"That'll be all, Mandy."

Mandy blinks and flashes her boss a surprised look. "Are you sure?"

"Yes. Mr. Jacobs is due in for his cleaning in ten minutes. I need you at your station to greet him and get him started on his paperwork."

"Um, right. Of course."

She sidles behind the chair and heads for the door.

Oh good, she's taking the gun.

"Mandy, leave the gun."

The receptionist wordlessly passes the weapon to the dentist. I hold my breath during the transfer. I assume—or at least, hope—the safety is engaged. But I don't really want to find out the hard way.

Mandy leaves, pulling the door silently shut behind her. Doctor Pridemore examines the gun for a few seconds before dropping it into the big patch pocket of her white lab coat. Then she leans back in her chair and looks at me and Victor, silently sizing us up.

While she's checking us out, I give her the once-over, too. She's probably in her early forties with dark, glossy hair that hits her shoulders and wide-set eyes. She's wearing a chunky red-pink color necklace and matching bracelet that look like they came out of the display case in her waiting room.

She smiles, and even though I'm expecting a set of pearly whites, the gleam of her teeth is otherworldly. I'll bet she uses that charcoal toothpaste, too.

Focus, I chide myself.

"So, what am I going to do with the two of you?"

It's clear this is a rhetorical question, so I keep my yap shut. I think I've done enough talking, what with the 'I'm her granddaughter' story that landed us in this pickle.

Victor, however, leans forward and stares intensely at the dentist. "I suggest you let us go."

She snorts. "Yeah, not happening. Your wife, girlfriend, whatever she is—"

"Fiancée."

"How sweet. Your fiancée here impersonated my

deceased patient's granddaughter. I'd like to know why."

Victor cuts his eyes toward me. I know what he's asking, but I don't have a good answer. Can we trust her? Probably not. But do we have a choice? Probably not.

"That's a fair question, Dr. Pridemore."

"Oh, call me Alexis. You're not patients, after all." Her breezy tone belies the grim truth of our situation.

"Alexis, then. Okay, it's true that I'm not your patient's granddaughter."

She circles her hand through the air in a clear instruction to speed it up.

"But I am Thyme Field. Your patient, whoever she really is, stole my identity. She was using my name and Social Security Number, and I'd like to know why." I echo her words back to her.

She's good, Alexis Pridemore is. I'm watching her face, ready to note any reaction. If I weren't, I would have missed it. She blinks, twice, but her expression never changes. After a silent moment, she shrugs.

"That's unfortunate—for you. But the good news for me is that you're already dead. That's how you ended up here, right? Your name's been added to the Death Index, and you're as good as a ghost. Which means, if you die, it won't register as so much as a blip.

I mean, aside from with your fiancé here. But his grief will be short-lived, as it were." She cackles at her pun, and it's a stark reminder of the gun weighing down her pocket.

"Sure, you could kill us," Victor agrees in a casual tone. Under the table, he's tightening his grip on my hand. "And Thyme's death might be easy to conceal, given the situation. But mine won't. I'm a reporter on assignment. My editor knows where I am, and she'll be concerned if I don't file a story by five o'clock."

This time, the dentist's mask slips. Her cheeks hollow out as she sucks in a breath. Time to land a one-two punch.

I nod. "And we're traveling with a police detective. He knows we're in this building right now, meeting with you. Your choices aren't quite as wide as you'd like to believe."

"I don't believe you."

"Suit yourself."

She stares at me. I can see her mouth working. She's gnawing on the inside of her lower lip—worried now.

Good.

Finally, she says, "Well. This isn't good. If you'll excuse me, I need to make some calls."

She pushes back her chair and removes the gun

from her pocket, training it on us as she edges her way toward the door. She exits quickly.

Victor's halfway out of his seat before the door's completely closed, but the sound of a lock clicking into place drains the speed out of his movements.

Still, he walks over to the door and jiggles the knob. It's no use. We're locked in.

CHAPTER 13

Sage

The man behind the counter is explaining the snowflake system to Rosemary. It's clear he's skating over the details, giving her a sketchy, incomplete description of how this convoluted local bartering program works.

"But you do also accept cash and credit cards, right?"

She turns toward me and arches an eyebrow. She's asked this question three times now. He keeps not hearing it. I'm beginning to think it's intentional.

He huffs out a breath, and I figure maybe I should try to get an answer.

I pitch my voice sweet and high, girlish and maybe a little bit helpless. I'm not proud of it, and I would never model the behavior in front of Skylar and Dylan. But Rosemary isn't getting anywhere.

"Sir? We're asking because we're obviously not from here. We're just passing through, and we wanted to get that ... um ... banana slicer for our sister. She's getting married tomorrow." *Maybe. Possibly. Probably not.*

"Ordinarily, sure. We don't get a lot of outsiders, but I can take payment from you. To tell you the truth, though, today's the First Friday Frenzy, so I really shouldn't. Besides, you'll get better deals if you go to the frenzy."

Rosemary shoots me a look that asks 'what the heck is the First Friday Frenzy,' as if I have some secret knowledge that she lacks. I shrug, and ask the clerk.

"And what's the frenzy? Sorry." I throw in a ditzy giggle.

"Oh, right. You're not from here. So, all this stuff is here on commission." He waves a hand over the display.

"Like in a resale store?"

"Exactly. All the stores in town operate this way.

And we all take snowflakes as well as, uh, regular payment."

Rosemary's eyes narrow, a sure sign that wheels are turning under her blonde topknot of hair. "So, the address listed under the price—is that where the consignor lives?"

"You got it, girlie!" He seems almost giddy at the fact that we're finally catching on.

"And the frenzy?" I reel him back to the question at hand.

"Right. So the first Friday of every month, starting at three o'clock, there's a … well, it's like a neighbor festival or community yard sale, I guess. Everyone rolls up their garage doors and sells their stuff at home. There's music and food and drink, and everyone slashes their asking prices. It's a party atmosphere. So, if you see something in a store, like the banana slicer, and the frenzy's coming up, you wait and buy it then."

"And today's the first Friday."

"Yup."

I check my watch. "So the frenzy starts in less than an hour?"

His eyes drift to the apple-shaped clock hanging on the wall. "You got it."

I turn to Rosemary. "So I guess we should go to 16 Frost Court if we want the slicer."

"But, now, hang on. At the frenzy, it's snowflakes only. No cash, no credit. It's simpler for the sellers."

That makes some sense. I unzip my wallet and dig out a twenty-dollar bill. "What's the exchange rate? Could you change a twenty for snowflakes?"

A ripple of discomfort crosses his face, but, after a second or two, he shrugs, dismissing it. "Sure, why not. Twenty bucks, let's see … that'll get you, uh, thirty snowflakes. The banana slicer is listed at four. Today, Marianne will probably let you have it for three. So you'll have plenty of snowflakes left to shop around elsewhere."

"Marianne?"

"Marianne Lewis, at 16 Frost Court. Tell her Trey sent you." He winks at me and reaches under the counter for a blue zippered vinyl envelope, the kind a person might keep cash in.

I hand over the twenty in exchange for a pile of pure white paper that looks and feels like Monopoly money. I examine one. There's the black outline of a snowflake in the middle. That's it. No wording. I assume he's given me thirty single snowflake bills, but we'll find out soon enough.

I shove them into the billfold and zip the wallet

back up just as Roman and Dave come into view on the street. Roman's hefting a white bakery bag and giving a thumb's up sign with his free hand. Perfect timing.

"Well, thanks, Trey, you've been really helpful."

"Sure thing. Maybe I'll see you girls at the frenzy. Everybody closes up shop early so us merchants can get in on the fun, too."

"Great. Listen, Trey, do you have a restroom I can use?" Rosemary smiles widely.

"Sure, down that long hallway. The door's on the left." He jerks a thumb toward the back of the store.

"I'll wait outside with the guys," I tell her. I'm more interested in the contents of that bag in Roman's hand than I am in using the facilities.

She nods and heads for the bathroom. I smile a goodbye at Trey and walk toward the door, nearly tripping over my untied shoelace.

I crouch to tie it as Trey's phone rings.

"Kitchen Kookery, this is Trey," he answers then listens as the person on the other end launches into what seems to be an urgent story. I can hear the high, fast cadence of a woman's voice, but not the words.

While I'm down here, I untie my other lace and refasten it, tighter. At this point, I might as well wait for Rosemary. And, okay, sure, I'm eavesdropping. I'll own it.

I stand up and catch Roman's eye through the window. I hold up a finger—*one minute*—and then turn and stroll toward the restroom.

"Police detective and a reporter? Identity theft? No, I haven't seen any detectives. Just a couple of girls passing through, asking how the barter system works …" Trey trails off and looks at me.

My heart thumps. Trey's caller is asking about us. And judging by Trey's reaction, it's not so that they can alert the welcome committee.

"Hey," he says, resting the phone receiver on his shoulder, "come here for a minute."

I break into a run and catch Rosemary as she's opening the bathroom door. I grab her by the elbow and pull her along with me while Trey drops the phone with a clatter and rushes out from behind the counter.

"What the—?" Rosemary begins to protest but, at the sight of the large, red-faced man barreling toward us, she stops mid-sentence and starts trucking along with me.

"I really hope there's a back door," I huff.

"Sweet Lord."

There is. And we burst through it into a narrow, tidy alleyway.

"Left or right?" I shout, scanning in both directions.

"Uh, left?"

Just then, we hear barking coming from the right. Roman, Dave, and Mona Lisa are standing at the end of the alley. The humans are wearing bemused expressions.

"Right," I counter, and we sprint toward our husbands.

I crane my neck to see if Trey is following us, but he's standing at the edge of his property, hands on his knees, trying to catch his breath.

I pour on a final burst of speed and launch myself into Roman's arms when I reach the end of the alley. Beside me, Dave's catching Rosemary while the dog circles at their ankles.

"What in the name of pastries is going on?" Dave asks.

CHAPTER 14

Rosemary

Sage and I don't waste the time trying to explain. We drag the guys (and the dog) around the corner and across the small park.

"Let's go down there." I point to a path that curves between two scrubby shrubs. It seems to lead away from the town's commercial center. I don't know where it ends up, but away from the shops and the people looking for us works for me. I plunge down the craggy trail.

Dave urges Mona Lisa past the shrubs without so

much as a sniff, and Roman and Sage crash along behind us.

Back east, where my sisters and I grew up, most of the mountain trails are wooded, bordered by lush trees and trickling springs. And at the shore, where my parents ran a resort that we've taken over, the beach path is dotted with sea grass and beach heather and fragrant blossoming trees. Out in Los Angeles, the scenic canyon trails Dave and I hike are rockier and drier, but not like this.

This path is nothing but dust lined with rocks—towering, dark gray rocks—and clods of dirt. It's arid and punishing.

So, when we round the second bend and find a slope that leads down to a shimmering blue, manmade lake surrounded by an arc-shaped residential development—colorful detached, single-families houses laid out in a pattern of four nesting horseshoe shapes, each slightly larger than the last, each with a patch of grass and a tree or two—my gasp is one of shock, not of mere surprise.

"What the devil is this place?" Roman says in a low voice.

Sage answers with a shrug. "Mirage, obviously."

"I don't think we've been out in the desert long enough to see a mirage." Dave makes this contribution to the conversation in a tone that suggests he thinks Sage is being serious and not a smart aleck.

I clamber down the hill and mount a boulder to squint at the ironwork sign that stretches above the street entrance to the neighborhood. The sign's design is a clear attempt to match the style of the vintage sign welcoming visitors to Snow City's small downtown. But this shiny sign is too perfect to be of the same era as the oxidized, weathered one in town. Its newness makes it easy to read the words: *'Welcome to Winter Lake Village.'*

I turn and climb back to the others. "It's not a mirage. It's Winter Lake Village."

"Winter Lake Village," Sage muses. "Wonder if one of those streets is Frost Court?"

"That's what I'm thinking, too. Do you still have the pile of mail?"

"Yeah, Thyme only took the letter from the dentist. Why?"

"At least one of those catalogues has a forwarding sticker with her address on it, right?" I recall the yellow label.

"Um, that's right. Several pieces of mail have those stickers." She paws through her bag.

"Give me any one."

She digs out a magazine and presses it into my hands, back side up.

I turn it over to check out the cover. It's a quarterly for knitting enthusiasts. This is definitely the fake Thyme's subscription. I turn it back to the address field and gently peel off the yellow sticker that bears Thyme's New York address. I lift the label from one corner with exquisite care, then I yank it off with a smooth motion.

Sage leans over my shoulder and we stare down at the address I've uncovered, the one that's printed on the magazine: *Thyme M. Field, 24 Holly Branch Court, Snow City, Arizona.* Despite my care, I've ripped off most of the original zip code with the label. But it hardly matters. I'm willing to bet … all my snowflakes … that Holly Branch Court and Frost Court are two of the four manicured streets clustered in Winter Lake Village.

The wind picks up, and I shiver. Until now, adrenaline and exertion have kept me warm. But standing still, up on this rock outcropping, with the breeze coming off the lake, I'm reminded that I may be in the Arizona desert, but this is the cold desert climate.

I stamp my feet to get the blood flowing again. "Come on. Let's go find Thyme's house."

~

We slip through the gate and split up. Four of us, four streets. I run to the center of the development, the smallest arcing street and check the sign: Icicle Court.

I jog to the next street and bump into Roman at the entrance. He's pointing his thumb behind him. "That's it."

I wave my arms overhead, and Dave and Sage head toward us. The four of us cluster at the entrance to Holly Branch Court and catch our breath. Mona Lisa strains on her leash, interested in the lake.

"So, this is the street. Now what?" Sage asks.

I glance at Dave. This part's about to get tricky. After all, he *is* an officer of the law. "Um, I think we should check out the fake Thyme's house."

"By 'check out,' I take it you mean 'break into'?" He raises both eyebrows and waits for my response.

I straighten my shoulders and hold my head high, the way my mother taught me, and fix him with an impassive look. "No, by 'check out,' I mean 'check out.' We don't know, the garage might be open or someone could be staying there—a relative or friend. Someone who can explain what's going on. Because, Thyme and Victor are in a jam now."

Dave's about to respond, but Roman beats him to it. "About that. Now, can you two tell us why we high-tailed it away from town, and away from both the van and your sister and Victor? If they're in trouble, shouldn't we go help them?"

It's a fair question.

Sage nods. "Someone—if I have to guess, probably the dentist—called the shopkeeper right as we were leaving. Whomever he was talking to said something about identity fraud, reporters, and police. The caller asked him if he'd seen any police detectives, and he said, no, then said he'd seen *us*. Then, he chased us, and you know the rest."

Dave scratches his left eyebrow.

This means he's analyzing information. If he tugs on his chin, he's working out how to break bad news. Cracking his knuckles means he's about to apologize. The man has an entire nonverbal language.

"We don't know that Thyme and Victor are *in trouble*. But it's clear they've stirred up a hornet's nest of some sort. So, at this point, it does make sense for the four of us to lie low and regroup, and the dead Thyme's house is as good a spot to do that as any."

I check my watch. "Glad we're in agreement. Now, let's hurry up and get off the street—the First Friday Frenzy starts in ten minutes."

"First Friday Frenzy?" Roman repeats.

Sage loops her arm through his. "Come on, we'll explain inside."

We bunch up into a tight knot of bodies and speed walk toward a small, cottage-style house with buttery yellow curtains in the front window and a large bronze 'No. 24' affixed to the creamy white front door.

Dave rings the doorbell while Sage and Roman go around to the back. I creep through the garden bed to check the garage door. I'm lying flat on my stomach in the driveway, trying to pry up the automatic door with my fingernails, when Dave gives up on the doorbell and starts hammering on the door.

The garage bay door is a lost cause. I brush myself off and head for the side yard, planning to walk around to the back to see if Sage and Roman are having better luck.

I trip over a loose stone and crash into a pair of large, wheeled bins. One for trash, one for recycling. My stumble sets off a domino effect. I hit the trash bin, which knocks into the recycling bin, which smashes into the glass window of a side door with a thunderous bang. The glass in the door cracks, a network of spiderwebs spreading across the pane.

Oops.

I jerk around to the street to see if my noisy clumsiness has attracted any unwanted attention, but there's not a soul out other than the four of us and the dog. I pause for a moment and eye the silent army of vehicles lining the street. Every home has a car parked on the street to the right of its driveway. At first, I'm puzzled, but then I remember the garage sale. The residents must move their cars out of their garages for the frenzy.

I frown at the white Lexus parked in front of the fake Thyme's house. Who moved it?

Before I can work out a theory, Dave's running toward me with Mona Lisa on his heels.

"What happened? Are you hurt?"

I shake my head and point to the side door and its broken window. "I'm fine, I just tripped over a rock. But, on the bright side, I think I found us a way in."

Sage and Roman appear on the side of a short hedge row.

"The back's locked up tight. What was that noise?"

"Your sister," Dave says, jerking a thumb in my direction.

I give a sheepish wave.

"I thought you were the klutzy Field?" Roman says to Sage.

"So did I." She giggles. "Are you okay?"

"Yeah. But listen, we might as well take advantage of my cloddishness. It's almost three."

Before anyone can object, I wrap the sleeve of my sweater around my fist and punch in the broken glass. I'm expecting a cascade of glass shards, but instead the whole pane slowly bends inward and falls to the floor inside the house in one piece.

"Neat," I breathe.

"Safety glass," Sage informs me. "Sure wish Linda Zaharee had that."

It takes me a minute to place the name. Oh, right, Linda Zaharee is the sports agent who tried to frame both Roman and his dad Chip for murder. At one point, she was holding Roman hostage, and Sage crashed a golf cart through her glassed-in porch.

"Let's do this inside," Dave suggests.

I feel around on the inside of the door until I locate the doorknob.

"Oh."

Everyone looks at me.

"It's, um, not locked." I ease my hand out of the now-paneless window and turn the doorknob from the outside. You know, like a normal human being.

To their credit, neither my husband nor my sister and Roman say a word.

I yank open the door and we step inside.

CHAPTER 15

Thyme

I waste who knows how many precious seconds staring dumbfounded at the locked door. Finally, I shake myself out of my daze and turn to Victor.

"Can you believe a dentist pulled a gun on us?"

"No, I actually can't. And now we're—what? —hostages?"

"Apparently. We're being held against our will at a dentist's office."

I consider banging my forehead against the table, but I can already feel a tension headache building. So I do the next best thing. I laugh. It starts out as a one-hundred-percent fake laugh, but it quickly turns into the real deal. Sure, it's gallows humor, but it's humor.

Victor's eyes go wide with worry. "Uh, Thyme? It'd be really helpful if you could keep it together."

Good thing I didn't opt for the head-banging route.

"Sorry, having a moment. I'm good now." I take out my phone and swipe to unlock the screen. I can't quite believe Dr. Pridemore didn't confiscate our phones, but I figure she likely doesn't have a ton of experience in hostage-taking.

His eyes flit to the door. "Hurry."

I'm already thumbing out the text to my sisters:

> Being held hostage by armed and dangerous dentist. DO NOT call police. Not sure who we can trust. Help.

I hit 'Send,' and then stare unblinkingly at the screen, willing Sage and Rosemary to respond.

Victor clicks his tongue against his teeth, just loud enough for me to hear. I drag my eyes away from the phone long enough to see what he wants.

"Help me move this." He gestures toward the solid-looking credenza pushed up against the far wall.

"What are you thinking—use it to block the door?"

He nods. "If nothing else, it'll buy us some time when she comes back."

I'm about to point out that I doubt the thing is bulletproof. But there's no harm in dragging it across the room and jamming it in front of the door. It's better than sitting here and waiting to be rescued … or killed.

I place my phone down on the table and hurry over to the credenza. As I bend my knees and prepare to hoist my end of the credenza, I glance up and to my right, through the window. The conference room we're trapped in is on the fourth floor on the back side of the building, so the window has a view of the HVAC system installed on a flat roof that covers the first three floors of the building.

I raise the piece of furniture all of an inch, then I let it go. Victor, who's lifted his side as well, isn't prepared for the heavy credenza to drop back to the floor.

"Ooof."

I wince. "Sorry."

He waves off my apology. "It's okay. But try to give me some warning next time."

"Mmm … right."

My focus is on the window, not our exchange. I

press my forehead against the pane and stare down at the lower roof, calculating and devising.

After a moment, he joins me at the window. "Uh-oh, wheels are turning. What're you thinking?"

I point down at the roof. "If we can get this window open, we can make the jump to that roof, easily."

He eyes the distance. "Only one of us is made of rubber, remember?"

I arch an eyebrow. "If you'd commit to doing the stretches I gave you, you'd be more flexible. But, I don't think you'll need to be particularly bendy to drop, what, ten feet?"

"Not a chance, Thyme. We could kill ourselves."

He's right. We could. But if we stay here a bonkers dentist could do the job for us.

"Besides, what do you plan to do once we're *on* the roof? It's got to be at least another thirty feet to the ground."

He's got a point. Before I can counter it, my phone vibrates on the table. I snatch it up.

"It's Rosemary," I tell him. "Here, read it over my shoulder."

He squeezes in close, and we peer down at the text:

OMG. They're looking for us. Hiding out at Fake Thyme's house. On our way.

"No," Victor and I moan in unison.

I twist my neck to meet his eyes. "They can't come here. That's playing into her hands."

"Call her."

I hesitate. "What if they hear me?"

"They won't if you keep your voice down. They'll probably think you're talking to me. Hurry."

I hit the telephone icon and place the call to Rosemary's cell phone. My eyes are glued to the door as I listen to the ringing. While I wait for Rosemary to pick up, Victor starts pushing the credenza toward the door, inches at a time.

"Thyme?" Rosemary's voice is raw with fear.

"Don't come here. You all need to stay far away from here. Please, promise me," I beg her.

"Thyme—"

I cut her off. "We don't have time to argue, Rosie. I think we've figured out a way out of the office."

Victor turns to stare at me. He shakes his head from side to side. No, no, no.

'It's okay,' I mouth. I have a new plan. It doesn't involve jumping. At least, not exactly.

"Don't do anything stupid," Rosemary orders me.

"We won't. What did you mean when you wrote that people are looking for you? Who?"

"I think that dentist is calling all over town asking people if they've seen us. Sage and I were in this weird kitchen store when she called the owner. Sage overheard his end of the conversation and we booked it out of there, but he chased us. The people in this town are weird. You should've seen the junk in that store."

I remember Dr. Pridemore's bizarre bazaar display. "Tell me about it. This dentist has a prize shelf in her waiting room with essential oils and handbags and all sorts of stuff."

Rosemary doesn't react to how strange this is. Instead, she asks, "Is she selling it?"

I think back for a moment. "I don't think so. I didn't see any prices, just—"

"—Let me guess, snowflake values."

"Wait, what are we doing? We can talk about this when I see you. Where are you anyway? Where is the fake Thyme's house?"

She rattles off an address and I type it into a text message to send to Victor so we'll have it. Then she says, "We ran here, along some trail. So the van's still in the lot."

"Too bad it's useless to me. You know, since I don't have the keys."

Imagine my surprise when she laughs. "Actually, if you can get to it, there's a spare key in an old mints tin. It's stuck to the right rear wheel well with a magnet."

For a moment, I can't even breathe. I stand there, stunned into silence. Finally, I squeak, "Are you serious?"

"Sure. When I cater events, I hire college kids to help. Sometimes they need to run back out to the truck to get supplies. I'm not giving a bunch of teenagers and twenty-somethings my keys; besides, I'm usually too busy to stop and deal with whatever they need. So I stick the spare key on the wheel well when I'm working an event, tell them where to find it if they need it, and then bring it inside with me when I get home."

"Okay, that's a decent system … except, why is it still stuck on your van now? Were you planning to hire caterers in Vegas?"

She huffs out an exasperated breath. "No, Thyme. I screwed up. I got home from working a corporate luncheon and started packing up for the trip right away. I forgot to remove it. But, hey, turns out to be lucky for you."

"Yeah. Lucky me." The luck part will be convincing Victor to go along with my scheme, but I don't tell her that.

"So, get the heck out of there and come straight to this little neighborhood where your imposter lived."

I hear Sage's voice in the background. A moment later, she's on the phone.

"Thyme? It's Sage. Are you really okay?"

"We're really okay," I assure her. But I know Sage well enough to know that a blanket statement won't truly satisfy her, so I go on, "I'm terrified, but unharmed."

"Rosemary says you have a plan to get out of there?"

"Yep," I chirp with far more confidence than I have. "We'll see you soon."

"Okay, Thyme, listen—be mindful."

I smile. I can't help it. Sage may not even realize it, but she's adopted one of our mother's classic parenting strategies. MJ never told us to 'be careful.' She thought it would stifle our exploration of the world. Instead, she exhorted us to 'be mindful' of the situations we were in and to pay attention to what was going on around us.

"I will," I promise.

"And make sure nobody follows you here. Oh, and one more thing, there's some neighborhood fair or something about to start. People are going to be milling around. So, maybe park just outside the entrance gates to the development and walk in. You'll blend in better on foot than you will driving a big catering truck."

"Sounds like a plan. Okay, I'm gonna go. I love you, and I'll see you soon. Tell Rosemary I love her, too."

"I will. Love you, Thyme."

She ends the call, and I turn to face Victor.

"We have a plan do we?"

"We do. And, no, it doesn't involve jumping to the roof and then to the ground."

"I'm all ears."

I inhale slowly, gathering my thoughts, and then start laying it out for him.

~

VICTOR STARES AT ME. "THIS SCHEME IS WORSE THAN the original plan."

A bubble of irritation floats up from my chest. I release it, allowing it to float away, before I respond.

"Our options are pretty limited. If we can't call the authorities for help, we're going to have to improvise."

He frowns and shifts his gaze away from my face. I'm right, he knows I'm right, but he doesn't like it. That's understandable. I don't like it, either.

After a long moment, he makes a grunting noise.

"If we're going to do this, let's be smart about it. Lay it all out one more time."

A wave of relief washes over me. He's onboard. And he has a far more analytical, detail-oriented mind than I do. He'll be able to find my harebrained ideas' weak spots, and maybe we can tighten them up before we execute.

I clap my hands together like a coach rallying her team. "Okay. First, I'm going to call the main number from my cell phone and tell Mandy I desperately need to use the bathroom. Presumably, she'll deal with us herself because Dr. Pridemore's busy, you know, being a dentist."

"Okay. So far, so good."

"We'll open the window, and then I'll squeeze myself into the credenza."

"You really think you'll fit?"

I crouch and open the doors. The shelves are wide and mostly empty, save for five or six file boxes that I can easily stack up and push to one side. Satisfied by my inspection, I close the doors and crane my neck to look up at him.

"Piece of cake," I tell him as I pop to my feet. "It would be for you, too, if you actually did those flexibility stretches, you know."

"You do realize I have five inches and fifty pounds on you, right?"

"Excuses."

He grins. "So when Mandy comes in, I'm going to tell her you panicked, went out the window, and jumped onto the roof where the HVAC system is."

"Right. Get her over to the window for a look. Then I'll burst out of the credenza and—"

The words die in my throat as footsteps approach in the hallway. The lock jiggles, and then the door swings open to reveal my least favorite dentist. She's gripping the gun two-handed, and her mouth is set in a grim, determined line.

"Thanks for your patience. I had to take care of Mr. Jones' cleaning. Here's a tip from me to you: your dental hygienist and dentist can always tell if the only time you floss is the morning of your appointment. Disgusting."

I *knew* it.

She goes on, "Now, it seems your friends are running around town, sticking their noses into things that are none of their business. That's rude."

I open my mouth to say—something, I don't even know what—but Victor beats me to it. "Whatever's going on here, you realize it's going to come out, right? You can't silence all of us."

"Right, right. And your editor's going to wonder when you don't file your story. I heard you the first time. Come on, Woodward and Bernstein, we're going on a little field trip." She gestures with the gun for us to walk toward her.

I really wish she'd stop waving that thing around. I glance at Victor, who gives me a slight nod, which I take to mean we'll have to improvise and come up with a new plan on the fly.

I clear my throat. "Where are we going?"

She answers in a put-upon voice. "The First Friday Frenzy. Well, I'm going. I guess I'll have to stash the two of you somewhere until I'm done. Now, move. Nice and slow. You first, then the fiancé. I obviously don't want to shoot either of you, but if you try to run, I won't have any choice."

I force my shaking legs into motion. As I walk past Victor, he reaches for my hand. He pulls me close and kisses my forehead.

The dentist snorts. "Touching."

I rise up on my toes and wrap my arms around his neck, hugging him close. "I love you," I whisper loudly.

"I love you more," he purrs, lowering his chin.

I press my forehead against his and whisper, more quietly this time, "Close the door behind you. Slam it in her face."

It's a risk, sure, but moving to a second location with an armed captor? That's a bigger one. Besides, I have to assume the gun's safety is engaged. After all, the woman is a dentist. She's educated, organized, and, presumably, she doesn't have a death wish.

He nods again, almost imperceptibly. It's a terrible plan, but it's the one we're going to have to go with.

"Okay, lovebirds, the tender moment's over. Get out there."

I swallow and turn away from Victor. My steps are measured and as steady as I can manage, which isn't very steady.

I hear the rustle of Victor's pants as he follows me toward the door. I cross the threshold and step out into the hallway. A second later, Victor steps out, and pulls the door closed behind him with a thunderous bang.

"Run!"

He could have saved his breath, because I'm already sprinting for the stairwell. He's right behind. We reach the stairs and push the heavy fire door open together. I hurtle myself down the metal stairs. Our shoes clang against the stairs, and the sound echoes off the walls, as we race down four flights.

My breath is ragged and my hands are shaking so badly I can't even grip the banister. Above us, a slam reverberates as the dentist pursues us. We've got a decent lead, though. We might actually make it out of here.

I launch myself, clear the final three stairs in a leap, and use my momentum to push down on the metal bar that opens the exit door.

I'm outside. The kiss of cool air is a gift.

I stumble out into the alleyway and keep running, arms and legs pumping. I won't stop until I reach Rosemary's catering van. I can hear Victor's feet slapping the pavement, a half-step behind me. As we near the van, he pours on a burst of speed and passes me.

He skids to a stop beside the rear right wheel and hunches over, blindly feeling for the mints tin. I throw a frantic glance behind me. Alexis Pridemore is trotting toward us, lab coat flapping. Two factors tilt in our favor: one, she's pocketed the gun; and two, her sensible heels are slowing her down some.

"Let me." I bump him out of my way and contort myself so I can see the underside of the wheel well.

Please, please, don't let the tin have been dislodged during the drive from California to Arizona.

I squint up at the wheel well and spot the shiny silver container. I pull it off and toss it to Victor while easing myself to standing.

He palms it, slides the lid open, and jams his thumb down on the unlock button. The van beeps obligingly.

I risk another backward glance, just in time to see Dr. Pridemore stop abruptly about ten feet away. She plants her feet in a wide-legged stance and reaches into her right pocket.

"She's going for her gun!"

Victor yanks the driver's side door open and jumps behind the wheel. I wrench the passenger door open and fling myself into the seat. He starts the engine while I fumble with my seatbelt.

"Where am I going?" he yells as the van rumbles to life.

"Just drive," I tell him as I watch the dentist in the side mirror. "Fast."

He peels out of the parking spot and careens toward the street. Dr. Pridemore raises the weapon, takes aim, and fires. The shot pings into the rear doors.

Victor jerks his head wildly and wrenches the steering wheel to the right. The tires squeal in response.

"She's shooting at us?"

I keep my eyes on the mirror as I answer him. "I think she's aiming for the rear tires, but she's not a very good shot."

"That's comforting ... I guess."

"It's better than the alternative. No, wait, she's getting in her car. Gun it—go!"

"Where?"

"Um, head toward the lake," I tell him as I fumble for my phone.

He floors the gas pedal, and the van lurches forward for a moment, then we rocket out of the commercial district and onto a residential road.

I'm trembling, awash in adrenaline, and it takes me three tries to unlock my phone. Finally, I navigate to my texts and find the one I sent to Victor while I was talking to Rosemary.

"We're looking for Winter Lake Village. They're at 24 Holly Branch Court, but we're supposed to leave the car on the outskirts of the neighborhood."

"We'll see if we have company when we get there. We're safer in here if that trigger-happy dentist is on the prowl."

His eyes drift up to the rearview mirror. Mine follow. The road is empty. There's nobody behind us ... yet.

CHAPTER 16

Sage

Rosemary's pacing, back and forth, back and forth, in front of Fake Thyme's mantle and gas fireplace. As Dad would say if he were here, she's wearing a path in the carpet.

"Anything?" I ask, even though I know the answer is no. I'm leaning against the wall all of about three feet away from her path. If her text notification sounds, I'll hear it.

Her eyes are glued to her phone's screen, as if her sheer concentration is enough to will a text from

Thyme into existence. She doesn't answer me or even give any indication that she heard me.

This isn't good. I leave her to her back-and-forth loop and go off in search of Dave and Roman. Mainly, Dave, to be honest. Because if anyone can deal with Rosemary in her intense state, I hope it's Dave.

I find them in the garage. If you can call the space a garage. *'Garage'* more or less suggests that the space is devoted to storing a vehicle, maybe some yard tools, a lawnmower, bicycles, holiday decorations—the usual. I suppose a workbench or other hobbyist gear would also fit within the traditional definition of a garage.

But this … is not that.

The space is spotless. The concrete floor is swept clean and painted a glossy white. The walls are lined floor to ceiling on three sides with shelving. And I'm not talking about the wire racks available at the big box home improvement stores. This place looks like a retail warehouse ate a smaller retail warehouse and vomited up the contents. These are heavy-duty shelves. They're deep, solid, and jam-packed with items. The center of the garage—the spot where one would typically find a car—holds a long white counter. A cash register and a rack full of bags anchors one end of the counter. I spot shelves behind the counter that hold neat stacks of cash register tape, a credit card reader, that stiff white paper used to wrap fragile items, bubble wrap, packing tape, clear tape, and twine. The counter is highlighted by warm recessed lighting.

"What in the …?" I trail off, unable to even form a suitable question.

Roman laughs. "Crazy, right?"

"Is this … Santa's workshop? Or wrapping station?" I finally manage.

Dave throws his hands up. "It might as well be. But, no, apparently it's Thyme's Time to Shop."

"Pardon?"

He edges past me and picks up a roll of preprinted stickers. The circular labels all read 'Thyme's Time to Shop' in a fussy pink script. The font, more than anything else related to the theft of my baby sister's identity, seems to be the ultimate affront.

"See?"

"Uh. Oh-kay?"

Roman makes a sweeping gesture that encompasses the shelving and its contents. "She was selling all this stuff. Out of her garage, apparently."

I survey the rows and rows of plastic tubs. "What is it?"

"Mainly leggings."

"Pardon?" I realize I sound like a hard-of-hearing

parrot, but my brain isn't quite able to take in the information it's receiving. It's kind of disorienting.

"Leggings. Really soft, colorful leggings." Roman's voice holds a hint of longing.

"You … want to wear leggings?"

We're still newlyweds. I'm not entirely sure how to handle this admission, confession, whatever it is—but I don't think he should be making it in front of our brother-in-law. I cut my eyes toward Dave, who is convulsing and red-faced. He's either choking or trying not to laugh.

"What? No. I'm just saying they feel like butter." Roman walks over to the nearest shelf, pulls a plastic tub out from its spot, and pries off the lid. He removes a pair of coral-and-gray ikat-printed leggings and thrusts them at me. "Here. Feel this."

Perplexed and oddly embarrassed, I stroke the fabric. Okay, he's right. It feels like butter. Or suede. Or sueded butter. Instantly, I want—no, need–to encase my legs with this material. Actually, what I want is to rub it against my cheek and sigh contentedly, but I restrain myself. I can't, however, quite suppress the moan of desire that escapes my lips.

"Um, what size are these?"

He snatches them back. "Focus, Sage."

I shake my head and snap back to reality. What's

wrong with me? My sister and her husband-to-be are being detained by a gun-wielding dentist who's set the whole town after us, and I'm lusting after a pair of *leggings?*

"Right." I nod briskly to let him know I've got myself in hand. He starts to shove the leggings back into the bin. "Hey, why don't you … you know, leave those on the counter. For later."

He shoots me a look of pure disdain, and I muster a shrug and a sheepish smile. You have to understand, the cloth feels like liquid, or clouds, or … unicorn fur.

"So, Fake Thyme must've been selling this crap out of her garage," Dave interjects.

I scan the shelves once more. "All of these bins are filled with leggings?"

"Most of them," Roman clarifies. "Some of them hold colorful plastic containers, exercise bands, workout DVDs, and plastic shake containers."

"Oh!"

My husband and my brother-in-law shoot me identical expressions of surprise. I guess the exclamation was more emphatic than I realized.

"Sorry, I know what that stuff is. Show me a box?"

Dave crosses the garage and removes a bin from the shelves closest to the bay door. He thumps it down on the counter.

I take off the lid and peer inside. "Mmm-hmm, just as I thought."

"Don't keep us in suspense, Sherlock," Roman cracks.

"Well, my dear Watson, it's elementary. This—," I pause dramatically and remove a glossy pamphlet/recipe book/workout program/journaling tool from the tub with a flourish, "—is the Fit-tastic Shape System guaranteed to mold you into the best version of you in forty-five days or your money back!"

Both men stare at me blankly—by which I mean, they show no spark of recognition, no soupçon of wry amusement, no abashed smile of acknowledgment that they, too, have, in a weak moment, been tempted by (or even fallen prey to) the glittery promises of the Fit-tastic Shape System monolith.

After a long, silent moment, I let the promotional material fall from my hand and flutter to the counter.

"Seriously? Nothing?"

Just then, the door from the house opens, and Rosemary enters the garage, still laser-focused on her phone, which answers the unasked question: she hasn't heard from Thyme.

She glances up from her phone and spots the brochure. "Fake Thyme was doing Fit-tastic Shape?"

"I think she was selling it," I tell her, tilting the box

filled with portion control containers and the workout gear toward her.

"Huh. That's a racket."

"Tell me about it." I can hear the smug note in my voice, but I can't help it. And to be honest, I'm not ashamed of it. I feel vindicated. Even if my husband and hers have no idea about the octopus-like reach of the Fit-tastic Shape devotees and their seductive promises, Rosemary knows. She *knows.*

"Ugh. Maybe one of her downlines killed her." Rosemary chuckles.

As far as I know, neither Rosemary nor Thyme has ever fallen sway to a multilevel marketing company. That's one benefit of being raised by hippies: the need to conform, to succumb to peer pressure is utterly nonexistent. Speaking for myself, I've never been remotely tempted by the promises of luxury cars, tropical vacations, and economic independence.

But. And it's a big but. I have loads of friends who've decided to supplement their family's income by selling essential oils or purses or natural cleaning supplies or, um, marital aids. And I dutifully present myself at myriad girls' nights or brunches or cocktail hours that I know full well come with an expectation that I'll buy something, anything.

And I do.

I peruse the catalog and find the second least expensive item (because the least expensive item is a glaring neon sign that screams *'I'm only doing this because we're friends'*). That's what I buy. No matter what it is. This is the reason I am the proud owner of a hand-painted ceramic cat dish (but no cat), a face cream made from rare mushrooms that smells like death, a bespoke passport holder, and … one set of Fit-tastic Shape Perfect Portion Boxes, still shrink-wrapped.

"She also sold leggings, apparently," I tell Rosemary. "Really soft leggings."

"Oh, yeah?"

"Yeah," Dave tells her, aiming a thumb toward the shelves near the light switch. "But proceed with caution. Your sister, Captain Ahab over here, has already fallen under the spell of that great white whale known as comfy leggings."

Rosemary snorts, and I roll my eyes. I know my own husband would sport a pair if I could find a size that fit his muscular golfer thighs. After a second, her laughter dies, and she narrows her eyes.

"Soft, colorful leggings?" she wants to know.

"Well, yeah," Dave says.

"Come here." I lead her to the shelves and open an extra-large bin to show her the mother lode.

"Hmm." She takes out a pair of leggings embossed with rainbow-colored foil butterflies and considers them. "Thyme has a bunch of these."

"She does?" Thyme has never struck me as a butterfly-type gal, but live and learn.

"Well, not *these* exact ones. Not this pattern. But this brand—MiMiMew."

"You're sure? This brand here?"

"Yeah, I'm sure. I guess we didn't tell you because you were on your honeymoon. After your wedding, Mom and Dad's … um … escort—"

"Prison guard?"

"Well, yeah. But turns out he's also a YouLift driver. Anyway, he drove us all to the airport, Me and Dave and Thyme and Victor—"

"Wait. With Mom and Dad, what, handcuffed in the third row?"

"Um … well, yeah."

"Rosemary!"

"Oh, come on, Sage. They didn't mind. It meant they got to spend more time with us."

"You're shameless."

"Anyway. He got my bag and Thyme's mixed up, and I didn't realize it until I got home and opened my bag to unpack. It was crammed full of—"

"MiMiMew leggings?" I venture.

"MiMiMew leggings."

As weird as this news is, it pales in comparison to what happens next: An air raid siren blares.

I jump. Dave drops a bin on his foot. And poor Mona Lisa wedges herself under the counter and covers her ears with her paws.

"Now what?" Rosemary shouts.

I'm beyond afraid to find out the answer to that question. But, by all appearances, of its own volition, Fake Thyme's automatic garage door begins its slow, jerky rise. I believe I'm going to learn the answer whether I want to or not.

Rosemary weaves her elbow under mine and pulls me close. I reach for Roman with my free hand, and Dave links up on the other side of Rosemary. I square my shoulders. If nothing else, we'll present a unified front to … whatever we're about to meet.

CHAPTER 17

Rosemary

To say that I'm utterly bewildered by what we found in the garage/showroom/warehouse is a huge understatement. The addition of a blaring air raid siren and a garage door that appears to be demonically possessed—or at least sentient—serve only to compound my befuddlement.

As the door inches higher, time seems to slow down. I'm suspended, waiting with equal parts dread and anticipation, for what will come. The good news is this drama is providing a measure of distraction from my concerns about Thyme and Victor.

To my left, Dave's gone rigid. He's at attention, alert and ready to spring into action at the first whiff of danger. To my right, Sage is sniffing the air, her nose twitching as if she's a rabbit. Mona Lisa mirrors her from her spot under the counter.

"Do you smell that?" Sage murmurs.

I inhale through my nose. It's not the scent of danger. It's something familiar ... sweet and salty and on the cusp of burnt. I can't place it, though.

"Is that kettle corn?" Roman ventures.

I think he's right. Why kettle corn? I can't imagine. But at this point, everything about Snow City points to the limitations of my imagination. All I can do is wait to see what happens next.

The garage door continues its upward journey, revealing a pair of feet encased in green plastic clogs just on the other side, at the top of the driveway. The owner of the feet is wearing gray sweatpants. The door jerks up another several inches. The gender and age of the clogs-wearer remain a mystery for now, but the air raid siren goes silent, which is a blessed relief—although in the sudden stillness, I realize that my ears are ringing.

I ignore the sensation and focus on the person in the driveway as the door rolls up the track. The visitor is a woman—barely more than a girl, really. She looks to be five or six years younger than I am. In her early twenties, if I have to guess.

She's wearing a faded t-shirt that reads *'Ask me about Baby Book Baskets!'* and her light pink hair is braided into two long plaits that hang over her shoulders. From behind a pair of round, oversized black-framed glasses, she blinks at the sight of us, arrayed behind the counter like a line of soldiers facing an advancing force.

She drops the plastic garage door clicker in her right hand. As the opener clatters to the driveway, she stares at us and screams.

"Shhh!" Sage admonishes her.

The screamer pays no attention, and continues to emit a loud, high-pitched wail. It might be worse than the air raid siren.

"Crap," Dave mutters. He shifts his weight as if he's considering breaking away and … what? Confronting her? Identifying himself as law enforcement?

I don't know what he has in mind, but I do know that we really don't need to draw more attention to ourselves. So, I break rank and zip forward out into the driveway before he has a chance. I bend and retrieve the door opener, pressing it into her palm. For a moment, I think she's paralyzed with shock, but eventually she closes her fist around the device and clamps her mouth shut, stopping the endless, Edvard Munch-worthy scream.

I smile encouragingly. "We didn't mean to startle you."

Her eyes, magnified behind her thick lenses, dart from me to the crew in the garage and back to me.

"Uh, it's okay. Sorry I yelped."

'Yelped' is a ridiculously benign description of the aural assault we just sustained, but I let that slide.

"No problem. Listen, why don't you come inside so we can talk?"

I scan the street. Apparently, the dreadful siren is the town's way of announcing the start of the First Friday Frenzy. All along Holly Branch Court, garage doors are raised and people are milling around in groups of three and four. The smell of kettle corn is explained by the presence of a red and white striped cart parked on the sidewalk. A sign on the cart's awning reads 'kettle corn, 2 snowflakes, hot dogs, 3 snowflakes.' On the other side of the street, a similar cart is set up, its vendor hawking lemonade for 1 snowflake.

Everyone in sight seems to be focused on the goods arrayed in the garages. From what I can see, the imposter Thyme's set up, while unique in my personal experience with suburban garages, fits right in. Directly across the street, I can see into a brightly lit, two-bay garage that looks as if a cardboard plant has exploded. Every square inch of space seems to be occupied by a precarious tower of corrugated cardboard boxes. The presumptive owner of the stuff is perched on a chair behind a white card table set up at the top of the driveway. A sign taped to the front lip of the table proclaims 'First Friday BOGO!'

Despite the bustling commerce, I feel exposed out here. I watch the young woman's face, hoping she won't take much convincing to retreat into the house with us.

She gnaws on her lower lip. "I dunno, you're going to miss the early birders if you aren't out here manning your table."

"It's okay," Sage assures her in her soothing nanny voice. "We'd really like to talk to you."

The woman's eyes are all over the place. Her nervous gaze darts around the garage and lands on Mona Lisa, who's watching the stranger with interest. I know that look: she's wondering if this lady's good for a treat—or, even better, a belly rub.

The answer appears to be yes, because the woman squeals in delight and makes a beeline for Mona Lisa.

I exchange glances with Dave, who hits a button on

the wall near the door leading to the house. The garage door begins its descent.

WITH MONA LISA IN THE LEAD, WE LURE THE WOMAN inside the house. Okay, *'lure'* sounds excessively creepy. We don't mean her any harm, of course. But we do need to keep a low profile, what with the armed dentists and irate shopkeepers out looking for us.

Our visitor is obviously familiar with the house. She heads straight for a white ceramic jar on the counter to the left of the stove, removes the lid, and peers inside.

"Oh, I thought there might be a few left in here," she says, speaking into the jar in an echoey voice. She reaches into the jar and takes out a bone-shaped biscuit. Mona Lisa's butt goes down on the floor in record time, as she sits and wags her tail in anticipation.

"May I?" the woman asks the entire room.

Of course. She has no idea who any of us are and which of us owns the dog.

"Sure," I say. "Her name's Mona Lisa."

The woman bends her knees. "Hi, Mona Lisa. Shake?"

Mona Lisa offers a paw, and is rewarded with a peanut butter dog treat and a pat on the head.

"Oh, no … is there a dog living here?" Sage looks around, worried that the dead fake Thyme has left a pet behind.

Our guest straightens to standing and smiles sadly. "No, the woman who lived here used to keep some biscuits on hand for my Paulie. Paulie's a bit high-strung, so I don't bring him out during the frenzy. Otherwise, he'd love to play with Mona Lisa. He likes dogs. Crowds of people, jockeying for the best deals … not so much."

I smile back. "Where are my manners? I'm Rosemary and this is my sister, Sage. The tall guy over by the fridge is her husband Roman, and this cutie is my husband Dave."

Dave, who's been eyeing the woman with what I can only describe as his 'cop look,' seems less than enthused by his introduction. Tough dog biscuits. He's going to intimidate her if he keeps staring at her that way. I need to soften his image. Besides, he *is* ridiculously cute. That's a fact.

The woman nods. "Nice to meet you all. Rosemary and Sage, ha, that's funny."

Sage blinks. "It is?"

"Sure. You know, Rosemary, Sage, and Thyme?"

She drops her gaze to the floor and continues in a subdued voice, "Oh, maybe you didn't know. The woman who lived here … her name was Thyme."

No doubt sensing her sadness, Mona Lisa cranes her neck and gives the woman's hand a long lick.

The woman giggles and lifts her head.

"I'm sorry about your friend," Sage says gently.

"Thanks. I can't quite believe she's gone."

She gets a distant look in her eyes, and I can tell she's lost in a memory.

After a moment, she pulls herself back to the present. "Anyway, I guess you're thinking about moving in here?"

"Um—"

Before Sage can tell her the truth, I jump in. "Is this house for sale? I didn't see a sign."

She cocks her head and gives me a curious look. "Of course not. Didn't anyone explain? The cooperative owns all the houses. You can live here rent-free, but no, you can't ever buy it."

"Right, of course," Roman interjects. "We're just, you know, not used to how it all works."

She nods. "I understand. It does take some getting used to. I think having mentors would be helpful to new residents. I've suggested it more than a few times. But some of the others vehemently oppose the idea."

"Why?" Sage asks.

A small shrug. "Too close to the structure of a lot of their systems, you know?"

No, I don't. I don't have the faintest idea what this woman is yammering about, but I nod anyway. "Sure, I can see that."

"So, Miss …" Dave begins in an obvious effort to prompt her to tell us her name.

And it works, too.

"Oh, geez, I'm such a ditz! I'm Car—Dora. It's nice to meet you all."

"Cardoora? That's an interesting name," Roman observes.

"Haha. No, it's just Dora. I get tongue tied sometimes." She blushes and looks away.

She's totally lying, and she's terrible at it. I catch the look that passes between Roman and Sage, which confirms that they share my view: there's exactly zero chance Dora is this woman's real name. In all likelihood, she's stolen some poor sap's identity, like her pal, dead, fake Thyme.

"So, *Dora,* why were you opening Thyme's garage door, anyway?"

She studies me for a second before answering. She's trying to decide if I emphasized her name to let her know I'm on to her. Yes, Dora, yes, I did.

After a beat, she says, "I wanted to sell some of her stuff for her. The First Friday Frenzy is the best time to move product. And you may have noticed, Thyme had a lot of it."

"That's an understatement," Roman offers.

She shrugs. "No more than most folks around here." She does the head tilt again. "Don't you?"

"Don't we what?" he counters.

"Have a stockpile? I mean, everyone who lives here is garage qualified. Obviously."

Garage qualified has a faint, familiar ring to it, but I can't quite place it. I'm still trying to recall where I heard it when Sage clears her throat.

"Well, that's kind of you to do that for your friend … er, her estate. But don't you have your own products to sell?" Sage nods at the message emblazoned across Dora's t-shirt. "The, um, baby book baskets?"

Dora looks down at her chest. "Oh, well, yeah, sorta."

Almost as if we've planned it, all four of us fall silent and wait. She scratches Mona Lisa behind the ear as she tells us her story.

"I was never really a big seller. My mom is my upline. So I bought exactly enough inventory to help her meet her quotas, you know? I actually managed to sell most of it off once my college friends started having kids. So, I usually kept Thyme company during the neighborhood sales. She always seemed sort of lonely."

"Didn't she have family?" Sage probes.

Dora flushes again. This time it's not embarrassment, it's fear. I can tell by the way her eyes dilate. Dave sees it, too.

"Something wrong, Dora?"

She inches away from us, pressing herself against the kitchen wall. "I don't know who you are or why you're here, but you're not recruits, are you? If you were, you'd know once you move to Snow City, you can't stay in touch with relatives on the outside. That's the rule."

We're all so busy exchanging perplexed looks that none of us notices when she grabs a knife out of the block on the counter and brandishes it at us with a shaking hand.

Dave takes a step forward, his hands outstretched and his movements deliberate.

Having been stabbed once upon a time, I'm not eager for him to spook her. And she seems easily spooked. She slices through the air with the knife like she's auditioning for a role in a slasher flick.

"Listen, Dora, it's okay. I'm a po—"

"Step back!" she shrieks at him, jabbing the knife toward him for emphasis.

"We aren't going to—"

His words are cut off by the sound of the doorbell ringing. Persistently. As if someone very impatient, or perhaps being chased by a maniacal dentist, is leaning on it.

Mona Lisa barks at the familiar sound and runs toward the front of the house.

"It's Thyme," I call over my shoulder as I follow the dog to the door.

In the kitchen, I can hear Dora stammering, "But … but … it can't be. Thyme's dead."

"We have a story to tell you. And I think you've got one for us," Sage tells her.

I unlock the door and fling it open. Thyme and Victor stumble inside, winded and wide-eyed, but seemingly unharmed.

"Am I ever glad to see you," I breathe.

My baby sister flings herself into my arms and breaks down sobbing.

CHAPTER 18

Thyme

I surprise myself with my emotional outburst. I mean, I *am* a graduate student in psychology. I'm fully onboard with the importance of accepting and allowing my feelings. But I guess I didn't realize the intensity of my feelings about being held against my will and then shot at—at least not until I see my big sister's worried face.

At which point, I'm not ashamed to admit, I dissolve into a puddle of tears.

Rosemary holds me, rubbing my back and making

shushing noises. I inhale the scent of her bergamot and lime body lotion and focus on the space between my in-breath and out-breath until I can get myself back under control.

My shuddering sobs slow, and then stop.

She pulls back, holding me at arm's length, and inspects my tear-stained face. "You okay?"

I nod.

"Okay. Then, let's get out of this doorway and close the door before someone sees us."

I nod again. Victor closes and locks the door, then he takes my hand. I lean against his shoulder, and the contact warms and re-energizes me instantly.

"Were you followed?" Rosemary directs the question to him.

He presses his lips together in a thin line. "I don't think so. But I can't be sure." His voice is strained, and his olive skin is unusually pale and ashen.

I realize that my dramatics are overshadowing his emotional reaction to our close call, and a wave of guilt splashes over me.

"Are you okay?" I ask him in a low voice.

"No. If I'm being honest, I'm scared half to death." His voice is steady and serious.

"That makes six of us," Rosemary says with an

understanding smile as she leads us toward the back of the house.

The adrenaline coursing through my body makes concentrating a challenge, but I try to take in the furnishings and decorating choices of the woman who stole my life, or at least my name. None of it feels like me. This makes sense, of course, because there's no reason why it should. And yet, I sort of expected to have some connection to the home environment of the woman who called herself Thyme Magnolia Field. I intellectually realize this makes no sense, but it disorients me all the same.

"Actually, it makes seven of us," Sage says from the doorway to the kitchen.

"Sage," I squeak, still high-strung, still a bit shaky.

"We were so worried, Thyme." She runs toward me and gathers me and Victor into a tight hug.

I relax into her embrace for a few quiet moments, then ask, "Seven?"

Dave and Roman appear behind her, flanking a woman I've never seen before. She seems friendly enough—young with a funky librarian vibe. For some reason, Dave is also holding a large kitchen knife.

"This is Dora," Dave explains. "She knew the fa— other Thyme. For a second, when she heard Thyme was coming, she thought you were a ghost, or maybe a zombie."

Dora ducks her head and laughs.

"Nope, I'm very much alive," I assure her. Then I remember my predicament and frown. "I mean, unofficially."

"For now," Victor adds grimly. "Alexis Pridemore doesn't seem to be the type to let things go. We're going to have to deal with her at some point."

Dora's mouth forms a little *'O'* of surprise, and she gasps. "You've tangled with Dr. Pridemore?"

"You could say that."

"This is bad. Really bad. She's fierce."

I eye the well-worn furniture in the living room off to the right. "Yeah, we noticed. Why don't we all have a seat and talk about it?"

She nods and heads for the corduroy recliner. She sinks into it and offers a shaky smile. "Thanks for the hand."

The rest of us arrange ourselves on the remaining seats. Victor and I squeeze into a small loveseat together. After the day we've had, I have no intention of letting him out of arm's reach. Rosemary, Dave, and Roman take the couch. Sage perches over the arm nearest Roman. I almost suggest she sit in the other recliner instead—she's going to break down the armrest that way. Then I remember this isn't my furniture, and its owner has no use for it anymore, and let the words die in my throat.

"Before Dora tells us about Dr. Pridemore, does anybody want to explain this massive yard sale?" Victor asks.

I chime in, "You probably didn't see it because you've been holed up in here, but it's bonkers. We parked the truck outside the entrance gate, like you suggested, so we got to see the Friday Frenzy up close. These people are serious about their garage sales. There's so much stuff."

"And some of these folks have commercial set-ups, with conveyer belts and scanners, the whole deal. It's wild," Roman says.

Judging by the blank expressions on their faces, we're doing a terrible job of conveying the surreal nature of the frenzy. I open my mouth to try again, but Roman jerks a thumb toward the back of the house.

"Yeah, we know. Go take a look at fake Thyme's garage."

"Um, okay?" I start to rise from the sofa, but Dora clears her throat, and I lower my butt back to the cushion.

"Can I tell you my story first? I think it'll clear at least some things up."

"Sure."

She exhales. "Thanks. But first, I want to be sure I'm understanding correctly: *you're* Thyme? The real Thyme Magnolia Field?"

"In the flesh."

She gives a frustrated little head shake. "I don't understand how this happened. They're only supposed to assign new identities from people who have already died. This is a pretty big mix up."

"Oh, you're preaching to the choir," I tell her. "We're supposed to be getting married tomorrow. And while I'm *not* dead, as you must know the pretend Thyme is."

"Right."

"Well, *her* death's been entered into some official database of deceased people. And guess who can't get a marriage license?"

"A dead woman," Dora says slowly. "Oh, no …"

"Bingo."

"What a mess," she moans. She plants her head in her hands and closes her eyes.

I happen to agree wholeheartedly, but I have to say I find Dora's reaction to be unusually strong. I mean, this disaster doesn't affect *her*. Does it?

I exchange silent looks with my sisters. Sage shrugs, and Rosemary shakes her head.

After a long pause, Dora lifts her head and meets my eyes. "This is really bad."

"SO, YOU ALL KNOW WHAT MULTI-LEVEL MARKETING IS, right?" Dora asks.

"Sure," I answer for everyone.

I know my sisters know about MLM. I mean, we're women. Living in the United States. With social media accounts. I assume their husbands have at least a passing familiarity with the concept. Victor is acquainted with the world of home-based, person-to-person sales through his economic reporting.

"Good."

Dora sits up a bit straighter, and I get the sense she's girding her loins, preparing to face down something or someone that's tormented her for a long time. That might sound presumptuous of me, but I'm good at reading people and discerning their internal reactions to external stimuli. In fact, this is the exact area of study I'm focusing on for my master's degree ... and maybe, someday, my doctorate. Even so, I have the feeling that Dora's story is going to blow my mind.

She doesn't disappoint.

"Most people don't get rich from signing up to sell an MLM line."

She says this as though it's a revelation and not common knowledge. Rosemary coughs, and I narrow my eyes. She's covering up a laugh.

"Right," I agree, hoping to prod her along.

"But some people do. Mainly, they make money from their downlines."

"Downlines?" Dave asks.

"The way it works is you sign up sellers under you, so you get credit for all their sales … and for all the sales of the people *they* sign up, who become their downlines. And so on," Rosemary breaks it down for him.

He taps the knife against his boot as he considers this. "So, it's a pyramid scheme?"

"Yes," my sisters say in unison.

At the same time, Dora says, "No."

Awkward.

Mainly to break the silence, I nod toward the kitchen knife in Dave's hand. "What's with the knife?"

Everyone in the room except for Victor shifts their gaze toward Dora. She grimaces. "Sorry about that." She turns to me. "I thought your sisters and their husbands were here to expose us. I panicked."

"Expose what?"

"I'm getting to that. But I am sorry that I grabbed the knife." She gnaws her lip, agitated and embarrassed.

"It's okay," Roman tells her kindly. "Nobody was hurt, and Dave's probably disarmed loads of people, right, Dave?"

"Definitely. Go ahead and tell your story, Dora."

She breathes out. "Right, thanks. Well, first, MLM businesses aren't pyramid schemes. They really aren't. The technical definition of a pyramid scheme is a business that doesn't actually involve distributing and selling a product. In a pyramid scheme, you make money by recruiting new members, and that's the *only* way you make money. As you can see from all the jam-packed garages, the people who live here sold—or tried to sell—products."

I think back to the display in the dentist's office and the signs Victor and I saw during our walk through the development. "So, now, you all sell this stuff to each other? But not for real money, for snowflakes?"

"Sort of, yeah. Everyone here is a refugee from a well-established MLM company."

"Refugee?" I can feel my mouth turning down. The word seems a bit dramatic for the situation.

But Dora's eyes are wide and earnest. "Oh, yes.

We're refugees. Snow City is the last resort for most of us. It was supposed to be a fresh start."

"Supposed to be—but wasn't?" Sage asks.

Dora nods. "I don't include myself in this. Like I said before, I'm only here because of my parents. They're in deep, but I'm not. Once they pass on, my older brother's going to get me out. I'll take my birth name back and start over. But most of these folks … they'll die here under assumed names."

"What is your real name?" I ask, curiosity getting the better of me.

"Carlie."

"Do you want us to call you Carlie instead?"

"No, no. That's sloppy. That could lead to mistakes. Exposure."

"I think that horse has already left the barn," Rosemary points out, not unkindly.

"Yeah, this is a disaster," Dora says glumly.

I pull her back to the conversation at hand. "So, refugees is a pretty loaded word. What are these people running from?"

"Their debt?" Sage guesses. "Did they overextend themselves financially buying products they weren't able to sell?"

"Yes and no. I mean, sure, anybody who's made their way to Snow City has disastrous personal finances. It's one of the reasons we don't deal in U.S. currency. Money is essentially worthless here. But, if a person wanted to get out from a bad financial situation, there are easier ways. You could take out a personal loan, declare bankruptcy, hit up a relative for a gift. No, the only people making their way to Snow City are in hiding from their MLM overlords."

"Overlords—you mean their uplines?" I want to be sure I'm understanding her.

"Well, sure, in some cases, it's their uplines, but it's not just that." She wrings her hands, struggling with how to word whatever it is she has to say. "You know how you can't simply leave a cult or a gang?"

"I don't have firsthand, personal knowledge, but, sure, I'm familiar with the concept."

"You can't just leave an MLM business either. Your upline will put extreme pressure on you to stay. They'll try to convince you that you can turn it all around—win that luxury SUV or qualify for the cruise or hit the bonuses—if you buy a little more inventory to have on hand and if you hustle a bit harder, sign up a few friends. Maybe convince someone to host an in-home or social media party for you? That's a quick way to pick up sales and potential new recruits in one fell swoop."

"So when a person makes noises about getting out, they're pulled deeper into the web," Sage observes.

"Exactly! And at some point, you look up, and you're in too deep to leave. The company owns you or that's how it feels, at least. There's no way out."

"So how did everyone get here?" I ask.

"They got a ride on Santa's Sleigh," she says cryptically.

"Excuse me?"

"It's a secret network run by escapees."

"So, it's like the Underground Railroad, but for people who want to leave sales organizations?" I can't keep the disdain out of my voice. I don't even really try.

"You can't understand unless you've been on the inside. If you complain, say you go online and search for 'how to quit my MLM,' you'll find forums, social media groups, whole communities dedicated to sharing tips and tricks for getting out, with success stories and everything."

"That's good," Sage says. "Then a person shouldn't have to resort to identity fraud."

"You'd think so, but you'd be wrong. They're *fake.* The support groups are a big hoax, run by a consortium of big power sellers from across a bunch of MLM companies. They want to root out the so-called bad apples, the sellers who are struggling and thinking about giving up. They coax personal information out of people, then they use it to get them even more firmly entrenched." Her voice is shaking and she pauses to gather herself.

Roman slips into the kitchen and pours a glass of water. He returns and presses it into her hands.

"Thanks." She takes a slow, small sip and resumes her story, "It doesn't always work, of course. Some people are just done. But if someone's really determined to leave and they can't convince them to stay, they hit them with a lawsuit—a defamation action based on their posts and emails. Sometimes, like in my mom's case, they fire with both barrels. The book company sued her for breach of contract *and* libel. And they began assessing a penalty for every month she didn't make her quota."

"Good gravy," Rosemary murmurs.

"Yeah. My parents owed them several million dollars by the end, which, of course, they didn't have. But it got worse. The books were in our garage and basement, right? All that inventory? I came home from school one day, and the locks had been changed. The company took possession of our *house* because they had a lien against the inventory. Basically any sales Mom made were earmarked to pay off the debt, and the unsold inventory was the collateral. It was something like that. So we were penniless, homeless, and being hounded by Mom's upline. That's when the Snow Queen stepped in and offered us a new life."

I'm sitting on the edge of the loveseat, spellbound, waiting to learn what happens next. "The Snow Queen?" I breathe.

"Nobody knows her real name. Everyone protects her identity. Because she's the only one who can connect you with Santa's Sleigh and bring you here, to Snow City. She assigns you a new name and gives you a place to live. In return, you give up your old life and agree to bring all your crap, er, inventory with you when you resettle. The town runs off a barter system powered by everyone's unsold products."

"Fascinating," Victor whispers. I glance over at him. His eyes are shining. I know that look: reporter with a story.

"Suspicious," Dave proclaims.

"Suspicious how?" Rosemary wants to know.

"What's in it for the Snow Queen? Are we to believe she does this out of the goodness of her heart?"

"Yes. Well, that's the legend, right? She clawed her way out from an iron-clad MLM agreement, started over, and rebuilt her life here, in a desolate, former ghost town."

"A ghost town, I knew it!" Victor crows.

Dora blinks at him, and then continues, "And then she dedicated herself to helping other people escape from the system. One by one, at great personal risk to herself."

"So that's the legend. What's the truth?" Sage asks.

"Most of that's probably at least half true. But, of course, she does get *something* out of it. She's the ultimate upline. Everyone she brings to town is her downline. Everyone *they* bring to town is also her downline. It all feeds up to the Snow Queen."

"What does?"

"Everything. She owns the entire town and everything in it."

"How?"

"When people agree to give up their old identities, she uses them to seed the town."

"What does that mean?"

"She ran up credit cards or took out loans to set up a fund to pay for groceries, utilities, things we need from the outside. And she keeps a little for herself."

"Wait a minute." Sage is doing that thing where she pinches the bridge of her nose. This is a sign that she's thinking, and the thoughts she's having are making her head want to explode. She stares at Dora. "You're telling me the plan to escape the iron grip of the MLM companies is … an MLM arrangement?"

Dora gives us a sad smile. "I think, technically, Snow City *does* meet the definition of a pyramid scheme. But it saved our lives, so nobody here's going to complain. Instead, people will defend it and the Snow Queen … to the death, if it comes to that."

CHAPTER 19

Sage

We leave Roman, Dave, and Victor to keep an eye on Dora while we have a quick sister confab in the kitchen.

"So what do you think of her story?" Thyme asks as we gather around the table tucked into other Thyme's breakfast nook.

"It sounds bananas. But it tracks with what we've seen in town," Rosemary says.

"Yeah, and the overflowing garages. I wish you could've been there while Victor and I were walking through the neighborhood."

"Believe us, we know. Come here and look at this," I tell her.

Thyme follows me to the garage.

Rosemary starts rummaging through the pantry instead. "I've already seen it. I'm going to try to scare us up an early dinner."

I fling open the door and gesture at the sales floor. Thyme steps down onto the concrete floor and gazes around at the shelves, dumbstruck.

"It's overwhelming, isn't it?" I say.

"What is all this stuff?" She walks over to the counter where we've left the Fit-tastic Shape System materials. "Fake Thyme was a Fit-tastic Shape Sherpa?"

"I think she did that on the side. Her main product was those leggings you like so much."

Thyme wrinkles her forehead at me. "What leggings?"

I reach for the nearest bin and pop it open. I toss her a pair of deep purple leggings patterned with gold and silver stars. "These MiMiMew things."

She examines the leggings. "Oh, these. I do have some, but I don't particularly care for them."

"Really? They're so soft."

"Yeah, they are. That makes them really comfortable as loungewear or to wear while you're running errands. But they're not well-suited for yoga or Pilates. They're *too* soft; they don't have enough stretch."

I'm not going to argue with her professional yogalates trainer opinion. But I do reach back into the tub and stroke the pair on top. *Like a cloud.* Meanwhile, Thyme seems to be having some sort of episode. She's staring down at the leggings in her hand like they've insulted her. Then she starts shaking her head from side to side and making these grunting sounds that aren't really words.

Maybe this is some sort of delayed shock reaction. She's had a grueling thirty-six hours.

I drop the bin and run to her side. "Thyme? Are you okay?"

She blows out a long breath. "Yeah, I … I think I know how these people got my name and Social Security Number."

I don't know what I expected her to say, but this isn't it.

"How?"

She lowers herself to the counter and sits on it, lotus-style, while she explains. "Right after I left school and started working with Cate Whittier-Clay, I was also picking up some hours at a yoga studio in Dumbo. Do you remember?"

"Sure." I do, vaguely. We were scrambling to come

up with the first payment on the debt our parents had tossed in our lap, and we were all taking every job that came our way. We were pretty desperate. Even so, Thyme's job in Brooklyn didn't last long. The commute was long and expensive, given the pittance she was earning, and it was hard to juggle her teaching schedule with the demands of her far more lucrative gig with Cate.

"So I only worked there for a few weeks, but one of the other instructors found out I was training Cate, and she became obsessed with getting me to give Cate a pair of these MiMiMew leggings." She waves a hand at the laden shelves.

"She was selling them?"

"Yeah, you know, that place didn't pay squat. Everyone there had a side hustle or two. And this woman—her name was Naomi Something or Other—she sold MiMiMew. She was relentless, too. Always inviting people to parties, but, when you got to her place, it would turn out to be a MiMiMew trunk show. The receptionist warned me about her on my very first day, so I tried to keep my distance. But she got it into her head that if Cate would wear MiMiMew leggings on the air, even just once, the sales would roll in, and she'd be set for life."

"Is that remotely true? Cate's an influencer like that?"

Thyme laughs. "No. She's a power broker. She deals in news, not this season's colors. Nobody follows her to see the latest trends. But Naomi was convinced all she had to do was get a pair of leggings into Cate's hands ... er, or onto her legs, to be precise."

"Did you give Cate a pair?"

She shoots me a look of sheer disbelief. "You've met her? What do you think?"

I know *I* wouldn't have the nerve to try it. "Um, I'm guessing not."

"Yeah, not a chance. I mean, I'm still kind of intimidated by Cate, but back then? Forget it. I was *terrified* of her. And I told Naomi that."

"She didn't accept it?"

"No, she didn't. First she gave me a pair, told me they were a gift from her to me."

"Awkward."

"I didn't really want them, but I also didn't want it to turn into a *thing,* so I took them, thanked her, and tossed them in my gym bag. I thought that would be the end of it, but it wasn't. Next, I found a pair in my locker at the studio. I gave them back to her, and they turned up in my locker again. I got a new lock, new combination, and started scheduling my classes to avoid her."

"Ugh."

"Right? And then, I got this package delivered to my apartment. It was a MiMiMew Consultant Starter Kit."

"You've got to be kidding me?"

"I wish. It was enormous. Mr. Doolittle had to help me carry it to my apartment. When I opened it, I just about died. There were *dozens* of pairs of leggings, branded bags with stickers and colorful tissue paper, all kinds of promotional items, and a bunch of MiMiMew brochures. And the log-in information for 'my' MiMiMew seller account. Oh, and an invoice for four thousand dollars, which showed that I'd prepaid by credit card."

She's pale and clammy from the memory. I can't imagine how she must've felt in the moment. There's no chance she had an extra four grand lying around.

"Oh, Thyme, what did you do?"

"First, I barfed. I mean that literally. Then I called the business headquarters and explained there'd been a mistake. It didn't go well, whoever signed me up knew my address, my social, they had a copy of my driver's license. MiMiMew corporate insisted I had to honor the agreement."

"Why didn't you ever tell us?"

"We'd just learned we had a half-million dollar debt to pay off, Sage. Everyone was sacrificing their dreams. Rosemary started working for that abysmal starlet, you'd left the accounting firm to be a glorified mother's helper to a stay-at-home mom—"

I interrupt to correct her, "Attachment parenting consultant. And going to work for Muffy turned out to be the best thing that ever happened to me. And I'll bet Rosemary would say the same thing about working for Amber."

"Sure, maybe in hindsight. But at the time, we were in full-blown crisis mode. I couldn't add another drama to the pot, so I was determined to resolve it myself. And I did … or, at least, I thought I did until today."

"Did you finally get them to rescind the contract?"

"Not right away. I disputed the charge on my card. The credit card company did an investigation and determined that my card number was keyed in manually by someone at a MiMiMew corporate office and not inputted through the signup portal online. That wasn't good enough for the company, but my bank did reverse the charges."

"So, you didn't have to pay for the starter kit. Did you send it back?"

"Twice. And I had to pay shipping, which wasn't cheap. Both times, they refused delivery and sent it back to me COD. So I guess I paid shipping four times. Finally, I decided to just keep the blasted leggings and file a fraud complaint with the state attorney general."

"What about Naomi?"

"Right, so by this point, I'd stopped teaching at the studio for unrelated reasons. I suspected she was behind it, but I couldn't prove it, you know?"

I nod. "Sure. But it's the most logical explanation."

"Yeah. Then I get a call from the studio. They discovered that someone had hacked into their internal database and 'harvested' some of the instructors' personnel files, including mine."

"Naomi."

"I thought so, too. They told me it was possible. In a weird twist, her file was deleted entirely, as if she'd never worked there. And she just … vanished."

She falls silent, and I try to piece this story about Naomi together with everything we've learned from Dora. It doesn't fit together cleanly, but it can't be a coincidence.

Footsteps sound in the hallway. I turn to see Rosemary standing in the doorway. "Are either of you hungry? I made pasta. It's the best I can do with the food on hand."

My stomach rumbles an affirmative answer, and my sisters laugh.

Thyme's laughter is short-lived, though. "I don't have much of an appetite, but I suppose we should eat while we can. It's only a matter of time before that demented dentist shows up. In fact, I'm surprised she hasn't already."

Just then, Dora appears over Rosemary's shoulder. The muscles in her neck are tensed, and her eyes stand out against her pale skin.

"Um, the guys asked me to let you know it looks like we have company. Sheriff Fellman and Doctor Pridemore just pulled up in front of the house."

I flash a look at Thyme. She's slightly green.

"Thyme?"

"Give me a second." She rests the backs of her hands on her knees, presses her thumbs and forefingers together, and then closes her eyes.

The rest of us stand stock still and watch her meditate. I hope she's asking the Universe for answers because we need all the help we can get at the moment.

Dora's words, that the townspeople will protect their queen *to the death,* ring in my ears. I sincerely hope our new friend is prone to melodrama.

CHAPTER 20

Rosemary

The announcement that the dentist has arrived with law enforcement in tow is obviously troubling. But—and, believe me, I know how this sounds—I'm feeling growly because I want to feed everyone, and now the pasta's going to get cold while we deal with Dr. Pridemore and the sheriff. Again, I realize how that sounds. Still, I eye the large pot of pasta as I hurry through the kitchen behind my sisters and Dora.

I can't help it. I show my love through cooking delicious, nutritious meals for my family. Dave always jokes that I have the soul of either a Jewish mother or an Italian grandma. But I know better. The need to nourish, to feed, cuts across gender, ethnic, and generational lines. And now these snowflakers, or whatever they are, are going to screw everything up.

Unless ... an idea begins to take shape.

We huddle around the window and peer out at the car parked behind Fake Thyme's Lexus. The dentist is ranting, making rapid-fire motions with both hands.

"At least she's lost the gun," Victor observes.

The sheriff's expression is flat, almost bored.

"Dora, tell me what you know about Sheriff Fellman," Dave says without ever taking his eyes off the window.

"Um, not much. He got caught up in Cured Cravings and—"

"Wait, what's that?"

"Oh, an MLM that sells cured meats, you know, like, bacon and beef jerky."

"The town sheriff has a garage full of bacon?" Roman asks in disbelief.

"Well, yeah."

My idea begins to jell, turning into something solid.

"Was he LE in his former life?" Dave brings the conversation back from its meaty detour.

"LE?"

"Law enforcement."

"Oh, yeah. He worked on the campus police force at some university. I don't know where, of course. But he's a real police officer. And even *he* couldn't get away from his company any other way."

"Hmm. So Doctor Pridemore was a dentist? What did she sell?" Victor asks. "You'd think a dentist would be too busy to have a side hustle."

"Okay, so she actually didn't sell anything. Her story is really sad," Dora says in a hushed tone.

"Can you give us the short version?" Thyme asks. "Presumably those two aren't going to sit there all afternoon."

"Sure. Here are the highlights, or, I guess, the lowlights: She was married to an artist. Her wife stayed home and took care of things on the domestic front while Dr. Pridemore earned the money. But her wife—I don't know her first name, sorry—wanted to contribute, so she started making and selling custom jewelry on commission. Apparently, her work was really special. She did these beautiful, one-of-a-kind pieces. And, eventually, a company called Natural Gems copied every single one of them for their line."

I'm a hard person to shock. I live and work in Hollywood, after all. But even I gasp. "That's horrid."

"It gets worse," Dora assures me.

"Oh, no, really?"

"Yeah. So, Dr. and Mrs. Pridemore sued Natural Gems. It should have been an open-and-shut case. They had dated pictures of works in progress, sketches, all sorts of customer testimonials and paperwork that showed that Natural Gems came out with their knockoffs *after* she created the pieces."

"But they lost," Sage guesses.

"Not only did they lose, but Natural Gems countersued and won. Doctor Pridemore appealed, and the case went on forever. I'm sure it cost a fortune. And then, Mrs. Pridemore got sick. Cancer. They dropped the appeal to focus on her treatment, but the cancer had metastasized. She died, and Natural Gems collected its judgment. Then it requested a, um, some kind of order that would have meant all Mrs. Pridemore's pieces had to be turned over and destroyed."

"They sought specific performance, most likely," Victor interjects in a low voice.

"Please tell me Dr. Pridemore didn't give up the jewelry," Thyme says, choking on her tears.

"No, she went on the run, and ended up here. She doesn't have any inventory of her own to sell, but she's one of us just the same."

"And she displays everyone else's stuff in her office,

right? That's what that case in the waiting room is for, isn't it?"

"That's right," Dora confirms.

We all fall silent and stare out the window at the sheriff and the tragic figure of the dentist. Quickly, before anyone can react, let alone object, I yank open the door and run outside toward the sheriff's car.

I can hear Dave calling my name as he flies down the sidewalk behind me, but I keep running until I reach the car. I raise my fist and tap on the passenger-side window. Alexis Pridemore gestures for the sheriff to lower the glass, and he does.

"May I help you?"

"Doctor Pridemore, my name is Rosemary Field, Thyme's sister. The real Thyme's sister. The guy stalking down the path, red-faced, is my long-suffering husband, Homicide Detective Dave Drummond. We'd like to invite you and Sheriff Fellman to join us for an early dinner. Nothing fancy, just pasta." I smile brightly.

The dentist narrows her eyes and considers my face. The sheriff leans over and inclines his head toward the house. "Who all's in there? Looks like a fair crowd of silhouettes at the window."

Dave joins me beside the car and shoots me a dark look that I pretend not to see. He greets the car's occupants with a nod. "Well, Sheriff, that'd be Thyme and Victor, whom the good dentist here already met, and Rosemary and Thyme's middle sister Sage and her husband Roman. We're also joined by a young lady named Dora, who let herself into the garage."

"It sounds like a regular dinner party," the sheriff muses.

"It will be if you stop by your house and pick up some pancetta for my sauce," I promise him.

He laughs and slaps his thigh, almost giddy. "What'd you say, doc? Will you be okay with these folks for a few minutes while I swing by my place?"

She looks like she's swallowed a lemon, but she nods. "Fine. But hurry." She pushes her door open without waiting for me to move. I jump back to avoid getting nailed in the stomach.

"Alexis?" Sheriff Fellman calls, leaning half out the window. "Your weapon, please."

He holds out his hand. She glares at him, and then she reaches into the pocket of her lab coat and removes a small handgun. She slaps it into his hand, and he tips his hat.

"Much obliged. I'll be back in a jiffy."

He zooms away from the curb, and Dave and I escort the dentist into the house.

As we reach the front door, Dave whispers, "Are you sure about this?"

I pretend to misunderstand the question. "Of course. I'm a professional caterer, remember? Shame on me if I can't stretch a pot of sauce and a mound of pasta to serve two additional guests."

His nostrils flare, and I know he knows I'm playing dumb on purpose. I reach over and give him a peck on the side of his mouth. "I have a plan," I whisper.

He plants a kiss right on my eyebrow. "That's what I'm worried about, Ro," he whispers back.

I have no response to this. How could I? It's so utterly justified.

So I smile cryptically and usher my baby sister's captor into the house.

CHAPTER 21

Thyme

I'm not sure how I'm supposed to feel about the fact that Rosemary has invited Dr. Pridemore and Sheriff Fellman to dinner. I guess I don't feel any particular way about the sheriff. I don't know him from Adam, and, crucially, he's never held me at gunpoint.

But Alexis Pridemore is a different story, and, despite the tearjerker of a story that Dora shared, I stiffen when she walks through the front door. Victor, in contrast, is the quintessential gracious host. I chalk it up to his experience interviewing reluctant or downright hostile subjects. I don't know any other way to account for it.

I mean, he ushers her to a seat, offers her a drink, and lends her his USB cord and brick to charge her cell phone. As a reminder, in case you forgot, this woman was *shooting* at us less than an hour ago. But, that's Victor. Big-hearted, expansive, and constitutionally incapable of holding a grudge.

I wish I could be so forgiving. I truly do. But I know myself. So, instead, I try to avoid the woman by volunteering to help Rosemary in the kitchen. Now, you might think there's not really much to do in the kitchen to prep for a pasta dinner. To you, I say, it's obvious *your* oldest sister isn't a chef.

Sage wisely gives the kitchen wide berth, choosing instead to polish the silver and set the dining room table. But Dora and I are Rosemary's staff, and Dora's getting an education. Right now, Rosemary has her warming the plates in the dishwasher because there's no other option and one simply can't serve eighty-nine-cent drugstore brand dried pasta on a cold plate.

Quelle horreur!

I'd give her some words of encouragement, but I'm pretty busy. See, I'm currently occupied softening butter over a candle. Yes, a candle. The toaster oven is occupied, and Fake Thyme doesn't own a microwave. I focus on the flame and the sunny yellow brick of butter and let all my thoughts seep out of me and drain away, like pasta water through the holes of a colander. I figure it's like a silent meditation retreat, only free.

"How's my bread?" Rosemary barks, doing a fair impression of a drill sergeant, and I'm forced to amend *'silent meditation retreat'* to *'boot camp.'*

But still, they have personal growth and discipline in common ... right?

As I contemplate the life choices that have led me to warming a stick of butter over an open flame, Victor's laughter carries in from the living room. I peek around the corner to see Dr. Pridemore trying to teach Mona Lisa to roll over.

I drag my attention back to the kitchen and, through the toaster oven's window, eyeball the quick-rising baguette Rosemary somehow created out of the meager contents of the Fake Thyme's pantry.

"It's just starting to turn golden brown."

"Thanks. Please keep an eye on it so it doesn't burn."

"Sure."

There's a knock at the front door, followed by male voices raised in greeting. The sheriff has arrived.

Doctor Pridemore glides into the kitchen with a plastic container in her hands.

"Here's the pancetta you wanted," she tells Rosemary.

"Great. Please put it on the counter somewhere."

She looks around for a clear spot, but Rosemary's cooking style involves using every square inch of space, not to mention all the bowls and pans in the kitchen. I move the bowl in which she'd mixed the bread dough from the counter to the sink.

"Here's a space," I say.

"Thanks." She sets the container down in the spot I created. Then she takes a few steps, hesitates, and turns back to me. "Just so you know, it wasn't anything personal—back at my office, I mean. I'm just … we're all just … trying to protect the town and each other."

Intellectually, I get it. I do. But I don't feel ready to let her off the hook.

Then her necklace catches my eye. In her office, I'd taken it for a mass-produced piece, the kind I'd seen at countless in-home jewelry parties. But now, I really look at it. It's clearly not an inexpensive trinket. Striated shades of red and pink run through the highly polished, variously sized stones.

I gesture toward her neck. "That's really pretty. Did your wife make it?"

She blinks, surprised, but recovers quickly. "Thanks. She did."

"What's the stone?"

"Tourmaline. It was Kimber's favorite. She always loved pink." Absently, she turns the matching bracelet on her left wrist, rubbing her fingers over the stones.

"Dora told us about what happened. I'm so sorry for all of it—your loss, of course, but also the theft and the fact that you had to deal with so much ugliness while you were grieving."

She swallows and furrows her brow. For a moment, I think she might cry, but she doesn't. "Thank you."

"We're not trying to make trouble for you—for any of you. But I need to get my life back."

Aside from marrying Victor, how am I supposed to take care of my banking or book a flight on an airline or do *anything* if the government believes I'm dead?

A constant stream of anxiety-producing worries about the minutiae of daily life swirls around in my mind. I keep pushing the noise to the side, trying to ignore it, but it's building. Soon, though, it'll be deafening, too loud to ignore. Great, now I think *I* might cry.

She's studying my face. "I understand. What I can't quite figure out is how the Snow Queen screwed up so badly. The fresh identities are supposed to come from deceased records. Yet, here you are."

"Here I am," I agree.

While we're talking, Rosemary heats the pancetta. I can't tell whether she's listening to our conversation, but I do have to give her credit: talking to Alexis Pridemore against the domestic backdrop of food preparation is easier than I thought it would be.

I turn to smile at my wise eldest sister just as the toaster oven chimes to signal that the bread is ready. Rosemary switches off the burner with a flourish and announces that dinner is served.

~

DINNER IS A LOUD AND BOISTEROUS EVENT. WE CRAM ourselves around the imposter's oval table, elbow to elbow, and pass the dishes family style. Dora, who knows where pretty much everything is in the house, unearths a bottle of red wine from the depths of the dining room cupboard.

As she uncorks it, I examine the label—*'Book Club Bordeaux, for delving in between the pages. Pairs well with smoldering romance, sweeping epics, and lush magical realism.'* There's a funky illustration of an open book with a circular stain across the page—a deep purple ring left by a wine glass. It's hip, and edgy, and, well, young.

"Hmm," I mutter as Roman pours the wine and passes the glasses around the table.

"Hmm, what?" Sage asks.

"I was wondering—how old was, you know, the other Thyme?"

Dora and Dr. Pridemore both turn toward the sheriff. "Keith would know," the dentist explains.

"She was in her late twenties or thereabouts. Maybe early thirties," he answers around a mouthful of spaghetti.

"What?" I sputter, narrowly avoiding a spit take with my Bordeaux.

Victor thumps me on the back.

"Thanks."

Everyone's staring at me. I take a small, careful sip of water and explain, "I envisioned her as older. I guess because of the dentures? And the fact that she's dead."

I mean, I can't be the only one. Can I?

A glance around the table confirms that my sisters look confused, as well. Beside me, Victor nods in agreement.

Doctor Pridemore chuckles and swirls her wine across in her glass. "I see. No, Thyme—er, the other

Thyme—had broken several teeth playing ice hockey. Her eventual plan was to get dental implants. The dentures were only supposed to be temporary until we could make the implants and schedule the surgery."

"Oh."

"Ice hockey?" Rosemary echoes. "Does the town have a team? Or a rink?"

"Oh, no," Dora explains. "Although she was trying to drum up interest. She used to drive to some ice center in Las Vegas to skate. When she could, she'd join the pick-up games that sprang up there."

"How did she die?" Dave asks.

"Car accident. It was early morning, and there was dense fog. She either lost control or couldn't see or both—she slammed into a concrete bridge pillar at high speed. The car burst into flames." Sheriff Fellman delivers this explanation in the flat monotone of a law enforcement officer struggling to remain detached.

We all fall silent for a moment while he gathers his thoughts.

He continues in a soft voice, almost too low to hear, "Her body was burned beyond recognition."

After another long pause, during which those of us not from Snow City give one another a series of meaningful looks that speak volumes, Dave clears his throat. "How did you identify the body, then, Sheriff?"

The sheriff focuses on picking apart a piece of baguette, sprinkling white crumbs all over his plate like snow.

"Well, I wasn't able to, exactly. But her purse was thrown clear from the vehicle, and her driver's license was in there. It wasn't too far of a leap from there."

I nod to myself and look away. My eyes fall on the living room window and the street beyond. "Wait. Isn't that her vehicle parked out front?"

The locals start shaking their heads. "You mean the Lexus?" Dora asks.

"Right."

"No, that's not hers. In fact, I'm not sure who it belongs to."

"What's it doing parked out there?"

Three sets of shoulders rise in shrugs. "I dunno," Dora adds.

"Well, how long's it been there?"

"Quite some time," Sheriff Fellman answers slowly. "At least since the day Thyme died. I remember seeing it sitting out there when I came by the house."

I clamp my lips together, hard, determined not to comment on the lax community policing.

Victor, however, has no such compunction. "Did you run the plates? Take a look through the windows?

Make sure there's not a corpse or a bomb or ten kilos of heroin in the cargo hold?"

Remember how I said he's such a sweetheart? He is —with one exception: he doesn't suffer fools gladly. And, frankly, this small-town sheriff's lack of curiosity about the abandoned SUV smacks of incompetency.

Sheriff Fellman has the decency to look abashed. He sticks a finger under the edge of his shirt collar and scratches his neck. "Well, no. I can't say I did any of that. I don't like to interface with the state and federal agencies any more than I absolutely have to. You know, we kinda need to stay off the radar."

"I understand that. I truly do," Dave assures him. "But, how can you protect your community if you can't —or won't—access the resources you need in order to do your job?"

The sheriff's eyes are glued to the tablecloth. He mumbles something indistinct.

I shift my attention to Dora. "Do you have any pictures of the other Thyme?"

She glances at Dr. Pridemore before she answers. "Um, maybe. Why?"

"Three reasons. One, I think I may know how she got my name—"

"She got it from the Snow Queen," Dora interrupts. "Remember, I told you all the names are assigned?"

"I remember. Let me ask you a question. When did the Snow Queen arrive? When did she open up Snow City to people looking for a way out?"

Dora looks up at the ceiling. By the way her eyelids bounce, I can tell she's counting silently.

"Wait—don't answer. Let me guess," I exclaim.

"Okay?"

"It would have been in the late spring/early summer four years ago."

Dora's eyes, already magnified by her glasses, grow enormous. "H-how did you know?"

"Thyme Field *is* the Snow Queen." I make the declaration with a touch more confidence than I have. "Thyme, are you sure?" Rosemary stage whispers.

"I'm pretty sure."

"So how'd she get your name?" Sage wants to know.

"Remember how I said Naomi used my name and personal information and signed me up as her downline without my permission?"

"Yes."

"And then she deleted herself from the employee database at the yoga studio and disappeared off the face of the earth?"

"Yeah?"

"That all happened the spring after Mom and Dad took off."

"Four years ago," Rosemary says slowly.

"Right. Four years ago."

"Wait. You think a former co-worker stole your identity *and* established the covert network for MLM members looking to escape? The Snow Queen was a twenty-something yoga instructor?" Alexis Pridemore's trying hard to connect the dots.

I push back my chair and stand up. "I do. *And* I think someone or something spooked her, made her think she was about to be found out, so she faked her death and fled town to protect all the rest of you. But it should be easy enough to confirm." I look around the table. "Let's go break into a Lexus."

CHAPTER 22

Sage

To everyone's great disappointment, we don't actually get to break into the SUV. Sheriff Fellman retrieves an unlocking kit from the trunk of his car, but before he can pull out the hook thingy, Dr. Pridemore tries the front passenger side door and, sure enough, it's unlocked.

Given that the woman pretending to be Thyme died more than three weeks ago, I assume anything of value or importance has long since been boosted from the vehicle. So I'm shocked when the sheriff emerges from the interior of the car with a cardboard box, the kind lawyers, bankers, and accountants use to store important documents.

"This was in the foot well," he announces, raising the box aloft as if it's a trophy of some kind.

The Friday Frenzy crowds have died down, but there are still pockets of people milling about in drive-ways and on porches enjoying the early evening air. The sun's last light hasn't quite faded from the sky but the stars are already winking overhead in the dusk.

"Keith, maybe we should take it back inside," Dave says as the sheriff rests the box on the hood of the SUV, apparently prepared to go through it right there out in the street.

Sheriff Fellman looks around, notes the neighbors, and jams the lid back on to the box. "Good idea."

He marches back up the sidewalk toward the front door and the eight of us trot along behind him.

We create an assembly line and clear the dishes from the dining room table and load the dishwasher in record time. Rosemary puts on a pot of coffee, and we all traipse back into the dining room to crowd around the table.

The sheriff lifts off the lid and sets it aside. I pop up on my tiptoes to peek inside the box. There's a small stack of manila folders. On top of the folders, sits a plain business-sized envelope with the name *Carlie* scrawled across it.

"Carlie, that's your real name, right?" Rosemary asks Dora.

She nods, open mouthed. "Yes ... but, I don't understand ... nobody knows that. I mean, I just told you an hour ago, but nobody in town knows."

"Well, the Snow Queen knows," Thyme points out.

"That's true," she breathes.

The sheriff hands her the envelope. "It's addressed to you, so I suppose you oughta be the one to read it."

She takes it gingerly, as if she's afraid it might burn her hands. We all watch as she slices it open with her fingernail and removes a single typed sheet. She scans it quickly, her eyes racing over the page. When she raises her head, her expression is unreadable, and her hands are trembling.

"Do you want to read it to us?" Thyme asks gently.

Dora nods, and then clears her throat:

"Dear Carlie,

Are you surprised I know your real name? You shouldn't be. I'm the one who gave you Dora as your new one. Yes, I'm the Snow Queen. I'll bet you're surprised, and you're probably wondering why I'm telling you this, right?

You're my closest friend in Snow City. I couldn't risk getting close to anyone in case they figured out that I'm the Snow Queen. But, you sensed how isolated I was, didn't you? You were so friendly that I decided to let you in … just a bit.

But now, something terrible has happened. I ran into someone from my old life in Phoenix last month. I pretended not to know her when she called me by my old name, but I think she's hired an investigator to look for me.

It's too dangerous for me to stay in Snow City. So I'm crowning you the new Snow Queen. The files in this box contain everything you need.

There's a folder for each resident, containing his or her original identity, a copy of their new identity, their MLM agreement, and inventory spreadsheets. As you know, Alexis Pridemore is a special case. Her folder contains the court papers from the lawsuits. Keep these documents under lock and key at all times.

As far as bringing in new residents, I think you should keep a low profile for a while. When the time is right, you'll find instructions for activating Santa's Sleigh in a large envelope in the bottom of the box.

The keys to the Lexus are in the junk drawer under my coffee maker. You can have the vehicle. I earned it as a MiMiMew rep but never drove it. It's been in storage until now.

I'm sorry I didn't get to say goodbye. Thanks for being my friend.

Thyme (Naomi)"

"I KNEW IT!" THYME PUMPS HER FIST. HER VICTORY IS short-lived because she notices the tears filling Dora's eyes. "I'm sorry about your, um, friend."

Dora chokes back a sob. "So do you think her accident wasn't an accident? Do you think this person from her past … k-k-killed her and made it look like a crash?"

She's addressing the sheriff and Dave, who both sort of shrug.

"It's possible," Dave allows. "Or it really was a tragic accident."

"Or—" Thyme begins, but Victor elbows her in the ribs, and she clamps her mouth shut.

"I didn't reach out to the county coroner because I didn't think there was any issue about who was in that car or how she died. So I doubt we'll ever know if she was a victim of foul play or just careless driving, Dora." The sheriff lowers his head and shakes it mournfully from side to side.

"I can't believe Thyme was the Snow Queen. She was so young," Dr. Pridemore muses.

Sheriff Fellman has a pained expression on his face. "Are you sure you're up for this job, Dora? There's no shame in saying you don't want to take up the mantle."

Dora's skin pales, and her breath is fast and shallow. "I don't … I don't know … if I don't, what will happen to us? To the town?" Her voice quakes with panic.

Neither the sheriff nor the dentist has an answer for her. But I think I might.

I jerk my head toward the kitchen, and Roman instantly understands.

"Sage and I will bring in the coffees."

"Thanks, Roman," Dave says distractedly.

We hurry out of the room before anyone can volunteer to help us.

CHAPTER 23

Rosemary

Sage thinks she's so sneaky, but I've been able to tell when she's up to mischief since I was six and she was four. She gets this light in her eyes, not a sparkle so much as a glow. And right now, her eyes are glowing. A second later, she and Roman scamper off to the kitchen.

I give them a twenty-second head start, then whisper to Dave, "I'm going to see if they need any help with the coffees."

He's absorbed in the documents being passed around the table, so he nods distractedly.

I wish I could get his full attention, because as sure as I am that Sage is up to something, I also have a feeling that Thyme's plotting and scheming. *She* gets a faraway stare when she's conniving. And she's definitely conniving.

But there's no way to communicate to Dave that he should keep an eye on Thyme without alerting everyone at the table. So I'm going to have to pick my battles. For now, I'll find out what Sage is planning. Then I'll worry about Thyme.

As I slip into the kitchen, I nod to myself, satisfied that I'm making the right call. I won't know until much later that I'm not. In fact, I'm making the exact wrong call.

"AH, ROSEMARY!" ROMAN YELPS WHEN HE SEES ME WALK into the kitchen.

Sage, who's over in the corner near the refrigerator whispering into her cell phone, wheels around, wide-eyed. Guilt is written on her face in the form of two bright red spots, high on her cheeks.

"Hi, you two," I chirp.

"Hey, help me with these, okay?" Roman asks,

moving between me and Sage to act as a shield and thrusting mugs full of coffee into my hands.

"Sure." I crane my neck to see around him. "Who're you talking to, Sage?"

She gives me an incredulous look and points to the phone as if to say she's a little busy at the moment.

"Who's she talking to, Roman? Tell me she's not on the phone with one of our parents."

Roman places a hand on each of my shoulders and stares unblinkingly into my eyes. "She is not on the phone with your parents. I promise you."

I relax incrementally. "Okay, thanks." I still want to know what she's doing, but I figure I can deliver these first two coffees and then return for more.

I walk into the dining room and place a mug in front of Dora and one in front of Dr. Pridemore. "I'll be back with the rest and the creamer and sugar. Well, sugar, at any rate. I doubt anyone would want to drink any creamer that's been sitting around here for who knows how long."

Nobody pays any particular attention to what I'm saying. Dave raises a hand and gives a little half-wave of acknowledgment, but everyone else's eyes are glued to the documents in front of them. And Thyme and Victor are holding up one of the folders as a screen and whispering behind it.

I huff out a breath and turn on my heel, back to the shenanigans in the kitchen.

"Thanks, Agent Morgan," Sage is cooing into the phone. "We'll wait for your call."

"Morgan? As in Internal Revenue Service SA-CIS Colin Morgan? The same Special Agent who busted Mom and Dad?"

"As a matter of fact, yes."

"And why is he calling you back?"

She smiles and picks up two coffee mugs from the counter. "Why don't I tell you all about it in the dining room so I only have to say it once?"

"Why don't you tell me now? Oh, I know. He pulled the strings to get them their furloughs for *your* wedding. You're trying to get him to do the same for Thyme, aren't you? But Sage, she said she didn't want them to come."

"First of all, Rosie, she didn't say she doesn't *want* them at her wedding, only that it's not feasible. There's a difference. And second of all, that's *not* why I called him."

I arch my right eyebrow and tap my toe against the tile to let her know I'll wait all day.

Roman scrubs a hand over his face. "Just tell her, Sage."

"Listen to your husband. He's a smart guy."

She shakes her head. "Fine, whatever. I'm just going to have to repeat it all for everyone else, but sure, why not? I called Agent Morgan to see if the IRS or maybe the Federal Trade Commission or maybe even the Department of Justice would be interested in building a case against a group of multi-level marketing companies who have so badly terrorized their representatives or sellers or whatever they are that these people have gone into hiding."

"Oh. That's genius."

She grins. "Isn't it? And, of course, he agreed that if the government were to undertake an investigation, the cooperating witnesses would all receive immunity from prosecution and clean identities. You know, under the witness protection program, not as the result of identity theft and fraud."

"This is great, Sage. I'm sorry I doubted you." My apology is one-hundred percent sincere, and I'm genuinely impressed by her quick thinking.

"It's okay, Rosie. I know you're being protective. But I'm glad you think it's a good idea."

"It's a *great* idea," Roman tells her.

"Do you think he's going to go for it? Morgan, I mean?"

She nods. “He’s onboard. He just needs to get all the approvals and follow proper procedure. But everyone in Snow City is going to be protected, and Thyme’ll get her life back.”

I want to give her a huge hug, but she’s holding two scalding hot coffees, and everyone knows she’s a klutz. So I settle for a quick shoulder squeeze and pick up two more mugs. “Great work, sis. Now, let’s go tell everyone the good news.”

“Let’s do it. Oh, *and* I didn’t ask, but Agent Morgan offered to arrange for Mom and Dad to at least attend the wedding, whenever it happens, via video feed. That’s better than missing it entirely, don’t you think?”

“I do.” I smile at her and we walk into the dining room side by side.

“Thyme, you’re never going to believe this—” she begins, then she stops abruptly. “Where’s Thyme?”

I scan the room. “And Victor?” I add.

“Oh, they said they had to get something from your van.” Doctor Pridemore waves vaguely toward the door. “It’s parked outside the gates. They’ll be back in a few minutes.”

I lock eyes with Dave. “Which file were they looking at right before they left?”

He surveys the table with his analytical, observant,

detecting gaze then meets my eyes. "I don't know. But whatever it was, they took it with them."

I sink into a chair. "They're not coming back, are they?"

Nobody answers. They don't have to. I know it's true.

CHAPTER 24

Thyme

Breathless and energized from the short run, Victor and I tumble into Rosemary's van.

"Do you want to drive?" he offers before he slides behind the steering wheel.

I smile at the question. Victor loves to drive, even in New York, he's comfortable behind the wheel. Meanwhile, driving's not really my jam—even if I pretend not to notice his white-knuckled grip on his armrests when I do take a turn.

"That's okay. If you don't mind driving, I can read

these more carefully on the way." I wave the envelope filled with Naomi's instructions for the new Snow Queen.

"Works for me." He settles himself in the driver's seat and turns the key in the ignition. Then he startles me with a loud laugh.

"You okay?"

"Yeah . . . imagining your sisters' reactions when they come out of the kitchen and find out that we left."

I bite down on my lower lip. "I'm picturing it, too, but for some reason, there's nothing funny about my version."

"Oh, it's a dark humor," he informs me. "You're going to be in so much trouble."

"Don't you mean *we're* going to be in so much trouble?"

"Nope, I mean you, baby sister Thyme."

He has a point—growing up with Rosemary and Sage was sort of like having three mothers. And not much has changed since childhood.

I shake it off. "They'll understand."

"*If* we're right, they'll understand," he reminds me.

"We're right."

"I guess we're about to find out." And with that, he shifts the catering van into 'Drive,' and we set off into the gathering darkness, headed for the Las Vegas Strip.

As if on cue, my phone blares to life, a flurry of text messages and phone calls. I tune out the dings, chirps, and ringtones.

Victor merges onto the highway that leads out of Snow City and spares a look for me. "You're gonna ignore your sisters, huh?"

"For now." Once we're closer to Vegas—when it's too late for them to try to stop us—I'll reach out to them and explain.

"Hmm."

I narrow my eyes at him and try to determine the meaning behind that *hmm*. After a moment, I abandon the effort and turn my focus to the files. He concentrates on the road.

After several minutes of silence, he asks "You really think she's still alive?"

"Don't you?"

"I don't know. If that wasn't *her* body in the car, whose was it?"

"Maybe this friend who recognized her down in Phoenix."

"So, she killed her and dumped the car? That's what you're positing, isn't it? There's a pretty big leap from identity theft to murder, babe."

I know. And it's a problem for my hunch. Leave it to Victor to poke at the weak spot.

"I know," I sigh.

"Unless ..."

I recognize that timbre in his voice. He gets it when he's chasing down a lead. "Unless what?"

"Unless Naomi's note is mostly true—her past caught up with her and she realized she couldn't, or maybe just didn't want to, stay in Snow City any longer, but she and this mystery person were on good terms. They left together and the wreck *was* an accident. But her friend was killed and Naomi survived."

"And she realized this was her chance to still move on? Just let everyone think the body was hers and get a fresh start somewhere?"

"That's the theory."

"Hmm."

He shifts his attention away from the road for a moment. "Hmm what?"

"It's pretty cold."

"She *was* the Snow Queen."

I chuckle at that. "And she'd have to be darn sure that nobody would question that the body was hers. Which means, this mystery person must've been a white woman about the same age and size as Naomi."

"A relative, maybe?"

A memory sparks in my brain, and I flip furiously through the pages in my lap, but I can't find the confirmation I'm looking for. "Man, I have this vague recollection that Naomi was a twin. Not identical, fraternal. At least, I think."

"That's a pretty specific vague memory," he points out.

"I know. Definitely someone at the yoga studio had a twin, I remember the topic coming up … but, it may not have been her."

"If only you had a supercomputer in your pocket."

"Yeah, if only," I agree distractedly. "Wait a minute …"

He shakes his head while I pull out my phone and fire up a search browser with Naomi's name and New York City as my search parameters. The third hit is gold.

"Victor, listen to this! This is from an article published two-and-a-half weeks ago. *'Jerome and Bettina Van Claus of Little Haven, Connecticut are issuing an appeal to the public to help them find their adult daughter, Adrianna Van Claus, age twenty-eight, who's been missing since last week. According to the Van Claus family's spokesperson, Adrianna disappeared while on a hiking trip through the Southwest. Her disappearance carries echoes of an earlier tragedy. Four years ago, in June, the Van Clauses' other daughter, Adrianna's fraternal twin, Naomi, vanished. Naomi was living and working in New York City at the time.*

Her disappearance remains unsolved. Anyone with information about' ... yada yada. Ugh, those poor parents."

"I can't believe it. So, Naomi is still alive?"

"Maybe. Probably."

"And you think you know where to find her?"

"I have an idea."

He nods toward the phone in my hand. "Call your sisters."

"I will. In a bit."

"Thyme, please do it now. If you don't, we both know they're going to go off on a wild-goose chase looking for us. And I, for one, am still holding out hope for a wedding tomorrow. It would be nice if your sisters and their husbands are still speaking to us and attend. Don't you think?"

I sigh deeply and roll my eyes like I'm a teenager on a sitcom, but he's right, and I know it. "Fine," I huff as I jab at my phone.

"Who're you calling, Sage?" he guesses.

"No, Rosemary."

"Really? That surprises me."

While I wait for the call to go through, I decide to give him a mini-education on his future sisters-in-law. "Calling Sage is the coward's way. I know it, and they both know it. If I call Rosemary, I'm owning my decisions. They'll be less likely to push back at me if I face down the dragon woman voluntarily."

"She's not a *dragon woman*. Come on, be fair."

"Okay, that's true. But she's pretty bossy."

"A time-honored characteristic of first-born children the world over," he tells me.

I'm about to respond when Rosemary picks up the call. I raise one finger to let Victor know.

"Thyme? Where *are* you?"

"Hi, Rosie. Listen, I'm sorry that Victor and I borrowed the van without asking you first, but—"

"You know this isn't about the van. Why did you run out?"

"We're following up a lead."

"A lead?"

"More like a hunch."

"Well, you left before Sage could tell you what she did. Hang on."

"No, wait—"

But she's already calling Sage to the phone.

"Hey, Thyme. Nice disappearing act."

"Sorry. Rosemary said you have news?"

"I reached out to Special Agent Morgan."

"Morgan? The guy from the IRS?"

At the sound of Colin Morgan's name, Victor cocks

his head and gives me an inquisitive look. I shrug. At this point, he knows as much as I do.

"Right. Him."

"Why? Oh, is this about Mom and Dad? Sage, I get it. I know family ties are important to you, but this really isn't the time. We need to—"

"It's not about Mom and Dad. The government has multiple open investigations into several of the MLM companies that these people in Snow City are hiding from."

I weigh this information. "I guess that's not completely unexpected."

"Right. There's a lot of deceptive business practices and some sketchy pyramid scheme stuff, snd some insurance scam that Morgan tried to explain, but I didn't really follow it. Oh, and tax evasion."

"There's *always* tax evasion."

That earns me a belly laugh from the former forensic accountant. "That's the truth. Anyway, Morgan's coordinating a response and a plan for Snow City. He called me back a few minutes ago. Everyone in town is going to get a real fresh start, without the stolen identities this time, in exchange for testifying against their companies or otherwise cooperating with the investigation."

"That's fantastic!"

"Right? And it means Dora doesn't have to take over as the new Snow Queen, which is good because she was right about the Snow Queen being at the top of a pyramid. The spreadsheets Naomi left behind are … instructive, to say the least. She was skimming so much money."

"How? I thought they only used snowflake bucks or whatever."

"Sure, amongst themselves. But she was their conduit to the outside world, which uses, you know, real money."

"Huh."

"What?"

I shake my head. "I'll tell you when I see you."

"Which will be when? Where *are* you, anyway?"

"We have to go back to Vegas to take care of something. Do you think you can borrow Dora's Lexus and meet us at the rental house in a few hours?"

"Um … probably. But, Thyme, what are you up to?"

"Maybe nothing. I'll know in a couple hours. Hey, can you fill Rosemary in on the plan? Kaythanksbye," I breathe in a rush and disconnect the call.

"Very brave facing down the dragon woman," Victor observes sarcastically.

"I wasn't *afraid* to tell her myself. I just didn't want to get dragged into a big, long conversation," I tell him.

"Mm-hmm. Anyway, why didn't you tell either of them about Adrianna?"

"I want to make sure I'm right first."

"And how are you planning to do that?"

"You'll see."

~

It's possible this was an error in judgment. I wobble and claw at Victor's arm to stay on my feet. Or at least a miscalculation.

He laughs, his eyes crinkling with amusement at my plight. "You sure about this?"

"Yes," I manage between clenched teeth. I'm not upset or anything, simply concentrating on staying upright.

He gently peels my fingers away from their death grip on his sleeve and puts my hand on the low wall. Then, like a big, fancy showoff, he spins around, executing a perfect figure eight and ending with a spray of ice.

"You're the boss. Let's get warmed up. Open skate ends in about five minutes."

"And then there's a pick-up hockey game? You're sure?"

"That's what the manager said while you were off renting the ice skates."

"Okay." I take a deep breath and tentatively let go of the wall. "Let's do this."

I glide forward and instantly lose my balance. My arms windmill wildly as my feet come out from under me. I land on my tailbone with a thud.

"Youch, that had to hurt," Victor says sympathetically as he reaches under my armpits and pulls me to my feet.

"Ack!"

I bobble, threatening to go right back down, and he steadies me.

"Here, stand in a snowplow. Like a novice skier, you know." He demonstrates putting his feet in the 'pizza slice' position taught on bunny hills everywhere.

I copy the move. I wouldn't say I'm steady, but at least I'm not teetering anymore.

"Great. Thanks."

A young girl in a glittery skating dress zooms past us and executes a flawless double axle.

Yay, another showoff.

"When did you say the last time you strapped on a pair of ice skates was?" Victor asks, concern wrinkling his forehead.

"I don't know, 1998, maybe?"

He does the math. "You haven't skated since you were six years old?"

"Give or take."

He rubs his forehead. "This is a terrible plan."

"It'll be fine. It's like riding a bike, right? I'll get the hang of it after a few spins around the rink. Anyway, this place is … distracting. That's not helping."

The only ice rink in Las Vegas that hosts pick-up hockey games is Louie Lou's Ice Palace. And the Ice Palace is everything you imagine a skating center right off the Strip would be. There are partially dressed cocktail waitresses gliding around the ice with heavy drink trays in one hand. A live band plays in front of the refreshment stand—their loud country rock competing with the pop blaring over the loudspeaker system. A bank of televisions plays, adding to the cacophony, each set displaying a different sports match. And then there's the magician working in the arcade.

The whole scene gives me an instant headache, and I'm steadfast in my belief that the chaos is contributing to my skating performance. Judging by Victor's wry smile, he's unconvinced.

"Okay," he says with clear reluctance. "Just … hold my hand."

I take his hand as instructed and then clutch his

wrist with my free hand. And then, he inelegantly hauls me around the outer edge of the rink, more or less dragging me as I cling to his arm and shuffle my feet ineffectively.

We make it all the way around without falling. I'm sweating and my heart is palpitating. But we did it. He deposits me on a wooden bench just outside the rink's surface. My thighs burn and my ankles ache.

But I grin up at him. "See, it's all muscle memory."

He leans in close and smiles at me. "You're such a lovable goofball."

I grab his head and pull his lips down to my mouth. After a long, hard kiss, I release him.

He laughs. "Thank goodness you're a better kisser than a skater."

"Hey!" I feign taking offense, but he's right. This isn't going to work.

"Do you want something to drink?"

"I'd love some water. And then I think I'd better put my street shoes on. I guess if she does show up for the hockey game we can confront her on solid ground—you know, after it's over."

"Excellent plan. I'll be back in a flash." He hurdles the wall and skates across the ice in the direction of the snack bar. As he speeds away, he turns and skates backward for a bit, waving at me.

So my future husband can skate. Good to know.

As I'm bending over and fumbling with my laces, a staticky voice cuts into the music. *"Open skates is over. Please clear the ice. Clear the ice for the adult hockey league. And remember, rail drinks are half-price until midnight."*

Rowdy laughter sounds over my shoulder, and I turn to see a group of men and women, clad in jerseys and gripping hockey sticks, clomping away from the dressing rooms, headed for the ice. I watch as they approach, focusing on the women, my eyes racing over their features. I stop on a familiar face. Upturned nose, dark eyebrows, bright blue eyes.

It's been several years, but the woman wearing jersey no. 8 could easily be Naomi. Maybe.

She turns her head to the side to say something to her friend, then she flashes a smile. She's missing three teeth.

I jump to my feet, forgetting that I'm wearing ice skates, one of which is unlaced.

"Hey, Naomi!"

She doesn't turn. But why should she? She abandoned that name years ago.

"Adrianna?" I shout. My voice is loud, desperate.

I can see her shoulders stiffen and she says something to the woman next to her. Her friend turns and studies my face then shakes her head.

I lunge. "Thyme? Hey, Thyme!"

She whips her head around as I pitch forward into the plexiglas wall that surrounds the rink. I lock eyes with her and ignore the hoots and laughter of her hockey friends.

Come on, Victor. Hurry back.

She blanches and breaks away from the crowd. She drops her stick, lowers her head, and pumps her arms like a speed skater.

Don't let her get away. Don't let her get away. The words drum out a rhythm in my head, propelling me forward.

I stumble onto the ice and, for lack of a better word, hurtle myself forward, arms and legs akimbo and completely out of control.

"Hey, lady!" a giant of man shouts as I smash into him.

"Sorry!" I ping-pong off him, hit the wall, and then ricochet back toward him.

In his anger, he does me an enormous favor. He stretches out his large, meaty hands and gives me a solid push.

The momentum propels me directly toward Naomi,

who turns to look over her shoulder, just in time to see me barreling down on her. I plow into her back, and we crash to the ice. She lands on her back, and I climb up on top of her, fueled entirely by adrenaline.

"Thyme?" she asks, staring into my face.

"That's right. It's me. The real Thyme."

She bucks her hips, and I slide off her, landing on my side. I can't let her get away. I reach out and catch a fistful of hockey jersey, yanking her back. With my other hand, I grab a hank of her hair and hold on tight.

"Fight! Fight! Fight! Fight!"

The chant goes up, loud and excited.

Naomi wriggles and kicks out her feet, catching me in the knee with a blade.

"Ooof." That hurts. A lot.

After that, things happen fast. The chanting turns into a roar. I headbutt Naomi, dazing her. I struggle to my knees and spot Victor skating toward us with a look of horrified disbelief etched across his face.

Distracted by the approach of my knight in rental skates, I'm caught off-guard when Naomi pops me right in the eye with a solid punch.

The sting is instant, and my eyes fill with water. I punch out blindly and connect with her jaw.

She lunges at me. At the same moment, someone in

the crowd launches their beer at us. Cold light beer rains down over our heads and shoulders.

Victor reaches us and crouches beside me. Before he can say a word, he's muscled aside by someone in a blue uniform.

I feel cold metal around my wrists and then hear the snap. "Ma'am, you're under arrest."

My only concern is whether Naomi's being arrested, too. To my relief, I see a set of handcuffs around her wrists. Victor's talking to the police, gesturing and pointing. I sag and let the police officer haul me across the ice.

Mission accomplished. Kinda, sorta?

CHAPTER 25

Sage

I peer through the metal bars at my sleeping sister like she's on display at the zoo. She's curled up on a metal-framed bed and wrapped in a thin gray blanket. Her long dark hair is matted, and even from this distance I can see the shiner Victor warned me about. An angry blue-black half-circle blooms under Thyme's left eye.

The corrections officer, a guy named Malone, smacks his baton against the bar, and the sound reverberates. Thyme jumps up, wide-eyed and dazed.

"Come on, Sleeping Beauty. Your sister here bailed you out."

Thyme meets my eyes reluctantly. "Hi. Ugh, I'm so stiff."

She drops into a full backbend. You know, as one does to work out the kinks. Finally she straightens, then lowers herself into a front split.

Officer Malone is agog.

"She's a yoga instructor," I explain.

"Well, she's sure not a hockey player." He chuckles at his own joke.

Thyme gets out of the split and does a series of stretches.

"You look like death," I tell her. It's true. Jumpsuit orange isn't her color. And the fluorescent lighting doesn't help.

"You should see the other gal," she cracks.

"That'd be hard. She was transferred into federal custody earlier this morning," Malone tells her.

Thyme's eyes widen in surprise, and then her hand flies up to cover the bruise. "Ow. She was?"

"She was. You did it. You caught her," I say.

She grins, and it's such an expression of pure joy that I bite back the lecture I planned to launch into.

Officer Malone has no such inhibitions. "Yes, you caught a felon, who's currently under suspicion for murder, through a combination of dumb luck and … well, just dumb luck. What you did was risky, foolish, and ought not to be repeated. Next time, call the police."

"Yes, sir." Thyme drops her eyes, abashed. But I think it's an act.

The guard seems satisfied, though. "Good. Now, get. I hear you have a wedding to get to." He presses a button on the wall, there's a loud click, and the door to her cell swings open.

She shuffles toward us, then freezes. "Wait. I do?"

I nod. "That's why I'm here. Victor's over at the clerk's office picking up the marriage license."

"Really? But, what about my … status?"

"Agent Morgan flew out last night to take Naomi Van Claus into custody. He worked his magic to get you declared undead."

"Yes!" She runs out of the cell and throws her arms around me in a hug. "I can't believe it!"

"Believe it. He's out in the waiting room with Roman. We invited him to stick around for the wedding. I assume that's okay?"

"Of course," she sings. Then she gets a stricken look. "Where's Rosemary? She's mad at me, isn't she?"

"No, she's not mad. She was distraught last night,

but she's over it. She's too busy to be mad. She's making your cake."

"She is?"

"She is," I confirm. "But she says since you chose to spend your last night as a single woman in the clink, she had to pick your flavors for you."

Thyme nods. "That seems fair. What did she decide to go with?"

"Lemon lavender cake with honeysuckle cream." I wonder if she'll catch the significance.

She does. "She used the same flavors for your cake —and hers."

"Just in different combinations. Because we're all different combinations of the same flavors." Or something like that.

She grins. "I love it."

I fling my arm around her. "Good. Now let's get out of here. We have our work cut out for us to make you look like a blushing bride and not a bruised and battered brawler."

The mention of her fight reminds her of Naomi and she stops walking again. "The guard said she's under suspicion for murder. Adrianna's?"

I sigh. I was hoping we could avoid this conversation, at least until after the nuptials.

"Yes. The government has a theory that Adrianna

helped her sister vanish four years ago and knew, in broad strokes, that she was living somewhere in Arizona. It's unclear whether they were splitting the money Naomi scammed out of the residents of Snow City or if Adrianna found out Naomi was profiting and demanded to be cut in. But there's some evidence that the so-called chance meeting in Phoenix was actually pre-arranged and went poorly." I shrug. "They'll know more if Naomi decides to talk."

"Could you imagine … killing your sister?" she shudders and wraps her arms around her midsection.

"No. Never." I smile at her. "But if we don't get you out of here and back to the house pronto, we're going to test whether Rosemary shares that view. Come on."

She rests her head against my shoulder briefly, then we walk out into the waiting room arm in arm. She smells faintly of stale beer.

CHAPTER 26

Rosemary

Sage and I stand in the master bedroom of the rental house and wait for Thyme to emerge from the bathroom. And wait.

Sage flashes me a worried look.

Finally, I cross the room and rap on the door. "Thyme? Do you need help?"

"No. I'll be out in a second."

A moment later, the door creaks open. Behind me, Sage catches her breath.

"You look beautiful," I breathe.

Thyme twirls, and the simple strapless dress she's

wearing flares out around her. She's arranged her thick dark hair in an elegant chignon at the nape of her neck. On her feet, are Sage's soft blue wedding shoes, satisfying both the something borrowed and something blue requirements.

"All we need is something new," Sage murmurs.

"And some concealer," Thyme counters, pointing to her black eye.

"It gives you character," I say, channeling our mother, and the three of us collapse on the bed in peals of laughter. According to Mary Jane, everything from chicken pox to intestinal distress to being caught in a mudslide builds character. There's zero doubt she wouldn't make the claim if she were here.

A knock on the bedroom door interrupts our antics.

"Are you Victor?" I demand.

"No," answers a female voice. It's Dr. Pridemore.

"Come in, then," Sage says, as we sit up and straighten our clothes.

She pokes her head in. "I don't want to interrupt, but I wanted to give you your gift early. You'll see why."

"Well, come in," Thyme says, gesturing.

Thyme and Victor's very small, family-only wedding, has doubled in size from four guests to eight:

Alexis Pridemore; Dora; Sheriff Fellman; and Agent Morgan are all joining us. Plus Mom and Dad by video. It's an unusual guest list, by any standards. But it seems fitting.

Now, the dentist walks into the room and presses a rectangular, hinged jewelry box into Thyme's hands. "This is from all of us at Snow City, for everything you —well, all of you—did for us."

Thyme raises the velvet-covered lid to reveal a light pink necklace nestled against the silk lining. She lifts it from the box with reverence. "Did Kimber make this?"

"Yes. It's more delicate than her usual work. She was drawn to bold designs. But she used a lighter hand for this. It's the only design Natural Gems didn't copy. I'd be honored if you'd wear it today?"

Thyme's free hand flutters to her bare neck, and she hands me the necklace. "Will you help me put it on, Rosie?"

"Of course."

I place the necklace around her neck and it settles in the hollow at the base of her throat. I clasp it and then turn her so I can see it. "It's perfect."

She looks at her reflection in the mirror hanging on the closet door. "It really is." She turns to embrace the dentist. "Thank you. I love it."

"And," Sage deadpans, "it draws one's eye away from your shiner."

"You know, I'm sure it's good luck to have a black eye on your wedding day," Doctor Pridemore ventures.

And suddenly, we're doubled over, cracking up again.

CHAPTER 27

Thyme

We originally planned to have the ceremony at the Japanese gardens outside the fanciest hotel resort on the Strip. But, when Colin Morgan manages to arrange for Mom and Dad to attend via video feed, we change our plans.

And the one place Victor manages to find on short notice that has the necessary satellite link and closed-circuit feed is the one, the only, Louie Lou's Ice Palace. I can't really complain about his choice of venues, given that I was in the county lockup while he did all the work.

The ceremony will not, thank heavens, take place on center ice. This is a good thing, because I'm still pretty banged up from last night's encounter at the rink. And, at least according to Sage, there's sawdust sprinkled across the blood and beer on the ice. That's me, classy all the way.

Sage and Rosemary and I are squeezed into the kitchen area behind the snack bar, waiting to hear the in-house country band strike up the first notes of Pachelbel's Canon in D.

"Is that it?" I whisper.

"I don't know," Rosemary whispers back, "I've never heard it played on a banjo before."

Sage snorts, loudly, and then blushes, belatedly covering her mouth with her hand. She stretches up on her toes and peeks through the doorway. "Let's just go, I see Victor looking around out there."

With a sister on each side of me, I step out onto the sticky wooden surface and smile at my soon-to-be husband, who's standing mere feet away, flanked by my brothers-in law, right in front of the Slushie machine.

"Hiya, Thyme!" I hear my dad's voice boom.

I glance up. He and my mom are beaming at me from each of the eight big-screen televisions on the wall. Mom waves enthusiastically. Mona Lisa, who's sleeping at Dave's feet, wakes up, barks once at the commotion, and then sinks back into doggie slumber.

Dora, Colin Morgan, Keith Fellman, and Alexis Pridemore are squeezed into the red vinyl bench seats of a melamine booth right up close to the action. They all stand up as we proceed down the aisle—sure, let's call it an aisle.

The officiant, whom I met for a hot twenty seconds back in the kitchen, was recommended by Officer Malone, the guard at the county lockup. She has all the necessary approvals to marry us, so who am I to argue?

She smiles and greets us as we arrange ourselves in front of her. I slip my hand into Victors. He squeezes his fingers around mine. This may not be the wedding I dreamed of as a little girl—after all, very few girls picture their big day going down at the snack bar of the ice skating rink where they got arrested the night before—but as far as I'm concerned, it's picture perfect.

My sisters are here. Rosemary, my rock and my guide. Sage, my soft heart and warm soul. And Victor. Smart, brave, sensitive Victor. I think I've loved him since the first day I met him, desperately seeking his sister, unwilling to rest until he found her. I smile up at him, pretending to listen to the words the officiant is reciting, while my heart swells with emotion.

"Sage, psst, *Sage!*" My mother is calling Sage's name in a loud stage whisper while waving her arms overhead like a flagger at the airport.

The officiant stops mid-sentence.

"Yes, Mom?" Sage's voice is neutral but I can see the tendons in her neck popping out.

"Does your sister have a black eye?"

"Yes, Mom."

"Listen, you soak a slice of apple in some witch hazel and—"

"Calendula tea, we know, Mom," Rosemary assures her. "We did, and we'll do another one after the wedding. Now, zip it!"

Mom shakes her head, affronted. And I start to giggle.

The officiant gives me a look of concern. "Do you need a minute?"

"No," I laugh. "Let's keep rolling."

"Actually," Victor interjects, "let's skip to the part where we say 'I do.' How's that sound to you, Thyme?"

A slow smile spreads across my face. "That's the best idea you've had yet, lover."

Two minutes later, Victor and I are wearing shiny new wedding bands, the officiant proclaims us Mrs.

Thyme Magnolia Field-Callais and Mr. Victor Callais, and I find myself on the receiving end of a long, warm kiss that promises to be the beginning of our next adventure.

I guess Victor had to fill out a new form to get our license. So I guess I'm also stuck with Magnolia. I probably would've missed my bizarro middle name anyway. I wonder which apartment he put down as our address?

Before I can ask him, the band strikes up Celine Dion's "My Heart Will Go On." I surmise from Mr. Callais' bemused expression that their choice is as much a surprise to him as it is to me.

The motley crew in the booth whoop and clap, and my sisters envelop me and Victor in a hug. Roman and Dave join us in the embrace, waking up Mona Lisa in the process. Dad is sobbing on the big screen, and Mom is rubbing his back.

It is, hands down and without a doubt, the best wedding I've ever attended.

CHAPTER 28

Three weeks later, New York

Thyme

I'm curled up with a mug of chai and a book when I hear Victor's footsteps in the hall outside our apartment. We decided to keep his place because it's two-hundred-square-feet larger than mine. I thought there'd be a longer adjustment, but this place already feels like home.

I mark my page and put down my book and my mug to greet my husband. He's been working pretty long hours since we got back from our road trip. As soon as he wrapped up the series on the economic state of small towns across the country, he pitched a series of articles focused on the pros and cons of multi-level marketing systems. And, as he's learning through interviews, there *are* benefits. Not everyone who gets involved in direct sales to their friends and family ends up a remorseless killer or bankrupt.

Plus, some of the products are pretty awesome, I allow, petting my MiMiMew legging-encased legs. Dora/Carlie helped the federal agents clear out Naomi's house and somehow convinced them to let her send me, Sage, and Rosemary each several pairs of cozy leggings out of the inventory.

Victor turns his key in the door as I'm walking to the entryway. I flick on the hall light and smile as he comes inside.

"Honey, I'm home!" he shouts, as he's shouted every one of the twenty-one days of our marriage.

And, as I've done every one of those twenty-one days, I wrap my arms around him in greeting and kiss him.

He kisses me back but doesn't return my embrace —probably because he's holding a large box in his hands.

"What's in the box?"

He grins at me. "Close your eyes."

I raise an eyebrow.

"Close 'em," he insists.

So I close my eyes and hold out my hands. "Is it a puppy?" The box is big, but it's not wriggling or barking.

He doesn't answer, but I can hear the rustle of tissue paper.

"Can I open them?"

"Not yet. Do you remember the first gift I ever gave you?"

"Mmm, well, you bought me an outfit to wear to your sister's fake funeral because we were on the run and I couldn't go home to get a change of clothes."

"Right, the traditional fake funeral attire gift. Do you remember the shoes?"

Do I remember the shoes? Of course, I remember the shoes. They were towering, sexy, expensive black high heels that I couldn't walk in. I ended up giving them to my octogenarian neighbor Mrs. Katzen, who rocked them with style. Please don't let him have replaced them. *Please.*

"I remember," I say, bracing myself.

"I guess I like buying you footwear."

Crud.

"Oh?"

"Okay, open your eyes."

Reluctantly, I do. And my gaze falls on the open

box. Nestled inside is a pair of snowy white, size 8, figure skates.

"Um?"

"Don't worry. They come with lessons. I thought by Christmas time, you might have your feet under you. We can skate under the tree at Rockefeller Center like tourists."

I smile at the image. "Well, thank you. These lessons you mentioned … who's the instructor?"

He brushes my bangs out of my face, "I was thinking I could teach you. I'm not bad on the ice."

"I noticed. And that'll work out just fine. Have I ever mentioned my fantasy starring an ice skating instructor?"

"I don't think you have. Why don't I get out of these work clothes and you can tell me all about it?"

I place the box on the counter and take my husband by the hand. This newlywed business is even more fun than I'd expected it to be.

ABOUT THE AUTHOR

USA Today bestselling author Melissa F. Miller was born in Pittsburgh, Pennsylvania. Although life and love led her to Philadelphia, Baltimore, Washington, D.C., and, ultimately, South Central Pennsylvania, she secretly still considers Pittsburgh home.

In college, she majored in English literature with concentrations in creative writing poetry and medieval literature and was stunned, upon graduation, to learn that there's not exactly a job market for such a degree. After working as an editor for several years, she returned to school to earn a law degree. She was that annoying girl who loved class and always raised her hand. She practiced law for fifteen years, including a stint as a clerk for a federal judge, nearly a decade as an attorney at major international law firms, and several years running a two-person law firm with her lawyer husband.

Now, powered by coffee, she writes mysteries and thrillers and homeschools her three children. When she's not writing, and sometimes when she is, Melissa travels around the country in an RV with her husband, her kids, and her cat.

Connect with me:

www.melissafmiller.com

Made in the
USA
Middletown, DE

75909369R00154